60p

Penguin Books
Penguin Modern Stories 11

D1494303

Penguin
Modern
Stories 11

Edited by Judith Burnley

Penguin Books

Penguin Books Ltd, Harmondsworth,
Middlesex, England
Penguin Books Australia Ltd, Ringwood,
Victoria, Australia

First published by Penguin Books 1972

Made and printed in Great Britain by
C. Nicholls & Company Ltd
Set in Monotype Baskerville

Contents

Kingsley Amis

Too Much Trouble 7
Dear Illusion 21

R. Prawer Jhabvala

Day of Decision 61
Two More under the
Indian Sun 82

David Zane Mairowitz

The Police 101
The Grace 109

Biographical Notes 137

All these stories are published
here for the first time in
this country.

Kingsley Amis

Too Much Trouble

Whenever Simpson takes a trip into the future in the TIOPEPE*, he gets through his official business as quickly as he can. He notes down the required information about political developments, scientific advances and the like, and then investigates the drinking habits of whichever age the authorities have had him sent to. It so happens that everybody on the time-project is keenly interested in that side of life: not only the Director (an expert on port), but Rabaiotti, my Assistant Engineer (chianti), Schneider, the Medical Officer (hock), me (beer), and Simpson himself (claret).

Most of the unofficial information gained in this way has proved to be of little more than academic interest. For instance, any serious wine-drinker would give his ears to sample the products of the New Grape, robonucleonically bred as a result of a chance discovery in an obscure Queensland vineyard and agreed by experts to be virtually identical with the basic, pristine strain attacked by phylloxera, the vine-louse, in the later nineteenth century and thought to have been wiped out for ever. But few of us would have the self-command necessary to keep us at the top of our tippling form in 2022, the year when the first New Grape wines will appear for sale. Just once or twice, on the other hand, Simpson has come back with something of vital importance.

* Temporal Integrator, Ordinal Predictor and Electronic Projection Equipment.

On Easter Tuesday, 1975, we received orders to report on how far the occupation of Mars was going to have gone by 1983. Within twenty-four hours we had everything lined up and shot Simpson forward eight years to the day.

In all technical respects, the operation could not have gone off better. Simpson reappeared in the receiver exactly on schedule, alive and well. Or fairly well. He looked haggard and in the depths of gloom, though that was nothing out of the ordinary after a time-trip. What startled us was that he had clearly been in a fight, his face battered and his clothing torn and dirty. Schneider gave him a tranquillizing shot and started to clean him up.

'What happened, man?' the Director demanded. 'What did they do to you?'

'Oh, this,' Simpson said, indicating his face. 'That's nothing. It's what I saw and heard ... Listen, all of you. We've got to sell up and buy an island somewhere. Somewhere they can't get at us.'

'You mean there's going to be an invasion or something?' Schneider asked.

Simpson shook his head slowly. 'Oh no. I'd have come across the results of anything like that in my trips to the 2000s, wouldn't I? No, it's just ... the life we're going to be leading. So soon. Give me a drink. A strong one.'

Schneider frowned, but made no other objection when I poured a stiff shot from the medicine-cupboard brandy bottle, and passed it to Simpson. He downed it in two gulps and, hesitantly at first, told us his tale.

At first sight, London seemed quite unchanged: demolition and construction works everywhere, vast unoccupied blocks already beginning to deteriorate, road repairs at 100-metre intervals with their familiar two-man work-gangs, barely moving crowds overflowing the pavements, and the traffic averaging perhaps three kilometres an hour, little if at all lower than the 1975 rate. About half of it consisted of private cars towing trailers piled with coloured plastic bins or containers, which was a novelty, but Simpson let it lie for the moment, and concentrated on making his way from his arrival point – a wc in the Oxford Circus public lavatory, pre-probed by the TIAMARIA* and found vacant for the necessary few seconds – down Regent Street to Piccadilly Circus.

Arrived there on foot no more than half an hour later, he again found a very recognizable scene. The Eros statue had gone, and this gave him a brief pang, but it was unexpectedly reassuring to find the drop-outs still there (so to speak) in their hundreds on the main traffic island and the surrounding pavements, sleeping and meditating and taking trips, twanging their electric *rebahbs* – the Moorish thing had really caught on, then – and playing their transwristors, chanting their traditional slogans in tribute to the victories of Greater Vietnam and the glorious dead of the London School of Economics, no doubt fornicating here and there among the discarded hypodermics and the piles of leaflets, assaulting passers-by and fighting the occasional policeman. Several times, Simpson heard American accents among the main stream of pedestrians, and concluded that this had remained a major stop on the sight-seeing route between Buckingham Palace and the Tower of London.

Within twenty minutes he had reached St James's Square and was climbing the steps of the London Library, the facilities of which had proved invaluable on several of his previous, longer-range trips. But this time the doors were closed and the building was evidently deserted. This was a considerable set-back. In a fit of anxious irritation he thumped vainly at the woodwork.

'Shut, mate,' called a cheerful voice behind him.

'So I see.' Simpson descended the steps and approached the speaker, a middle-aged man in overalls who, cigarette in mouth, was leaning against the door of a car parked at the kerb. 'Do you happen to know why?'

* Temporal Inspection Apparatus and Meteorological-Astronomical-Regional-Interrelation Assessor.

'Know why? You forgotten what day it is?'

'Wednesday. What about it?'

'What about it? It's *Easter* Wednesday. Don't expect anything to be open today, do you? Where've you been, anyhow?'

'Oh, abroad. Only got back this morning.'

'Where abroad? Same everywhere, I thought, bar Israel.'

'I've been in space, too,' Simpson said, improvising hastily. 'You know, Mars and so on.'

'Oh, yeah.' The man lost interest at once.

'Do I understand you to say *everything*'s shut? All the libraries and reading-rooms, all that?'

'That's right. It's the Easter slack period, see. Good Wednesday through to Easter Friday and then the week-end. As usual.'

Simpson was shocked and shaken. The ordinary six-day Easter holiday, from Good Thursday to Easter Tuesday, was fair and reasonable, but this was insane.

'So nothing'll be open before Monday morning.'

'Tuesday afternoon. Chum, you really have been in space, haven't you?'

'Sorry . . . Look, where can I buy a newspaper?'

'A *newspaper*?' The stranger reacted as if Simpson had in-quired about the purchase of an elephant. 'In the slack period?'

'Oh yes. So I'd have to wait for that until . . . today week.'

'You'd get a *News-Standard* then, yeah. If you want a daily it'll be tomorrow week. It must be, let's see, the *Times-Guardian*'s turn. That's right, it was the *Express-Telegraph* last week, the week before Easter, rather.'

'Thanks,' Simpson said dully. He was striving to think how he could gain access to some public source of informa-tion before his time was up and he had to return. 'Er . . . I've got a report to write for my firm. In a hurry. About, well, recent events. Is there anywhere at all, any agency, any government department, research centre, emergency ser-vice that might . . . ?'

The man was staring at Simpson and smiling broadly, with the expression of a contemporary garage mechanic, say, telling a customer that the spare part for his car had not turned up, but much intensified. It was obviously a rare and delicious experience for him to have found somebody so well qualified to be informed that he could not get what he wanted anywhere on earth (and no doubt on the planets, too). 'There's nothing, friend,' he said finally. 'Nothing at all. Think yourself lucky you haven't got a broken leg, eh?'

'And no drinks.' Simpson had thought aloud.

'Now, drinks, that's a different matter,' the stranger said, his manner growing perceptibly warmer. 'The pubs are open – Sunday hours, of course. In fact, I was thinking of dropping in for a pint myself. There's a place just up there, before you get to Jermyn Street. Care to join me?'

Simpson accepted with some relief, an emotion that changed to alarm when he realized, a minute later, that the pub in question was one he often used himself. It would be highly embarrassing to meet the 1983 Simpson in there. Then reason returned: he had only to remember to steer clear of the area when this day came round for the second time in his life, and all, or at least that much, would be well.

He exchanged names with his companion, who was called Ernie Mullins and said he worked in a vegetable factory.

'Oh, really?' Simpson said. 'What, er, what side of it are you on?'

'Vending. Outlet apparatus inspector.'

'I see. Whereabouts is this?'

'South-West Area. Leatherhead. It's not much of a job I've got, but it means a big part of Fetch-and-Carry's off my mind.'

Simpson did not like to question such a clearly basic concept as Fetch-and-Carry. Instead, he asked: 'I suppose you get a fair amount of custom out there, these days?'

'Yes, pretty fair. On a full working day we get nearly 200,000, which is over half a million in a full working week. A lot more than that before the slack periods, of course.

And the second week in December's murder, when they're buying for all that time ahead.'

'That many customers in Leatherhead?' Simpson inquired with careful casualness.

'Well, there are six million people in the South-West Area now, don't forget. I think we're overloaded myself. People ought to have bigger deep-freezes, so they could stock up for three months instead of three weeks. But there's not the room. Here we are.'

They were about to enter the pub when its door was jerked open from the inside and three struggling men began to emerge. One of them (a powerful pig-faced character who turned out to be the landlord, and to whom Simpson took an instant dislike) was trying to expel another (a long-haired, heavily-bearded person of about forty) with some assistance from the third (a near-replica of Ernie Mullins). All three were shouting angrily.

'Fascist pig!' the bearded man yelled. 'Power-structure élitist!'

'Get bloody lost! Get back to your sit-in!' This was the landlord. 'You can't treat me like your Board of Governors!'

'You irrelevant authoritarian! You pathetic oligarch!'

'Can't you read?' the third man demanded, pointing to a sign above the doorway that proclaimed: *No Students Alowed.*

'Of course he can't read, Joe, don't make me laugh, he's a student, isn't he? Now, you, take yourself off back to your boycott before I get cross! Ernie, give us a hand.'

Not very willingly, Ernie gave a hand, and in no time, still bawling accusations of fascism, pathos and irrelevance, the bearded man was reeling off towards the square. Simpson was introduced to the landlord, who nodded and went back into his house, and to Joe, who shook hands amiably and suggested a pint on him.

The bar of the pub was superficially as Simpson remembered it, but he soon saw that the counter was lined with dispensing machines of various sorts, past which a thick queue was laboriously shuffling. He went along behind Joe and Ernie, and was eventually handed a large plastic beaker. When the time came, Joe put some coins into a slot on a machine marked BITTER, collected three small packets from an aperture in it, and handed one each to the other two. He led them past other machines labelled MILD, STOUT, SCOTCH, GIN, VODKER – from the last-named three stubby pipes emerged – PORK PIE, SOSSIDGE, HAM SANGWIDGE and CRISPS. At the end of the counter, Joe took three smaller packets from a dispenser, doled out two of these as before, and nearly filled his beaker with what proved to be plain water. When the others had done the same, the trio moved away from the counter into the middle of a considerable crowd of drinkers, all standing: there was nowhere to sit down.

Joe and Ernie, followed by Simpson, dropped their larger packets unopened into their beakers. In a few seconds they had dissolved, wrapping and all, producing a clear lightish-brown liquid. The smaller packets went in similarly, and a foamy head formed.

'Cheers,' Joe said.

'Let's be lucky,' Ernie said.

'All the best,' Simpson said tentatively.

This proved acceptable and they drank. The 'bitter' was bland, by no means unpalatable, and without either much resemblance to the beer Simpson was used to or any particular character of its own. (He told us it bore very much the same relation to our bitter as powdered coffee to coffee.)

'Well, what do you think of it?' Ernie asked, but before Simpson could reply a sort of altercation had broken out at the bar.

'Do something about it, then!' an elderly man was repeatedly shouting at the landlord, who after a time switched off the miniature television set he had been watching and waddled impatiently up to the counter.

'Give over, can't you?' he said. 'What can I do?'

13

'Repair the bloody thing! I want vodka and I'm going to have vodka!'

'Not this week you're not! The machine's broke and that's that!'

'Replace the bloody unit, then!' the elderly man yelled. 'Or get a mechanic on to it!'

'You off your rocker? What's a mechanic? And how can I replace it now? Look, you take a gin on the house and pipe down.'

This was evidently thought suitable, and the hubbub died away. Simpson turned to his companions.

'Bad management, running out of vodka in the middle of a holiday.'

'Oh, he's not run out,' Joe said. 'Just the dispensing unit gone. Might happen to anybody.'

'You mean there's plenty of the stuff around, but it isn't coming through to the tap? Well, why can't he take it from the bottle or the tank or whatever it is? That wouldn't be any –'

'Too much trouble, mate. You can't expect him to do that.'

'Good God! He's got a pretty soft life, that landlord, hasn't he?'

'Has he hell! Think of Fetch-and-Carry in a place like this.'

'Fetch-and-Carry?' Though he had heard the phrase already, Simpson was now comparatively relaxed and off his guard, and for a moment he revealed his complete bewilderment.

Joe and Ernie looked at each other and seemed to make up their minds. Ernie spoke. 'You've been inside, Simmy, haven't you? You can tell us.'

Simpson in his turn came to a decision. 'Yes.'

'Course you have. Nothing to be ashamed of. Goes on all the time. The wife's brother, he was in eleven years. It's the strain, see. Treat you all right, did they?'

'Not too bad.' (Neither then, nor later, did Simpson establish what he had been inside, whether gaol or madhouse or some new-fashioned place of confinement.)

'So they ought. Well, you'll be needing to know about Fetch-and-Carry. Where are you going to live?'

'Oh . . . just round here.'

'Fine, you'll be South-West Area, then. The thing is, draw up your week's timetable and stick to it. Mondays do your burnable rubbish out at the Coulsdon dump. That'll take you the morning and some of the afternoon. Fill in the rest of the time with your shoes or the cleaners' or your fancy shopping. Tuesday take your unburnables down to Mitcham, then fetch your meat from Epsom or your fish from Weybridge or your booze from Ascot, if you can afford any. Wednesdays you'll want to do the Post Office, and that's where Joe comes in. He's in the sw GPO at Staines.'

'It's not such a bad trip as it sounds,' Joe said. 'We're pretty organized there. Shouldn't take you more than a couple of hours to sort out your mail and any telegrams, and then you can get straight to your telephone period. I'll fix that for you.'

Simpson looked his incomprehension.

'It's easy enough. You go to your booth, see, and you take your incoming calls first is the best way to handle it. After that you make your outgoings.'

'What's happened to private phones?'

'Oh, that was all stopped. They were always going wrong, and more people kept wanting one, and it was too much trouble driving out just to do the one job. The big offices and that, they run their own booth systems. Under licence from us, of course.'

'Then . . . the whole system of services has packed up?'

'They're trying to do away with what's left of it, yeah.'

'Same with things like milk? Laundry? Newspapers?'

'Same with everything, Simmy, mate. Thursdays and Fridays, now, when they bring out the dailies, you'll find it's a good chance to pick 'em up at the Area newsagent in

Woking, between your calls at Leatherhead and Ascot, say, about 1.30 or 2.'

'But, I mean, what about repairs and so on? You can't take a whole television set or washing machine back to the shop just because some tiny thing's gone wrong.'

'Oh, can't you? That's what a lot of the Fetch-and-Carry's about today. The places stay open over the slack, see, because they're all automated. The guv'nor here'll be off to Norwood with his vodka machine before he opens tomorrow. Not for repairs, though. Pick up a new one.'

'But that's completely uneconomic.'

'Maybe it is, but it's what you do. Only way you can save trouble.'

Simpson tried to think. 'So it comes down to this. You do very little actual work, but you spend all your free time doing the things for yourself that it's too much trouble for other people to do for you.'

'You learn quick. That's just how it goes. Only way they can get you to take trouble. We caught on to it first – you know, the British. Then everywhere else went the same road. We led the way there.'

'We would,' Simpson said through his teeth.

A silence fell between the three, though there was quite enough ambient noise from the other drinkers. Wearily, Simpson drained his beaker, and the smooth denatured taste faded at once from his mouth. A thought struggled to the surface of his mind.

'Can you get wine these days?' he asked.

'Plenty,' Ernie said. 'Burgundy, claret, hock, all that. I don't go for it myself, but it's easy enough. You pick up your wine-cakes from Ascot, stick 'em in a jug when you get home, add water, and in five minutes – '

'Wine-cakes! Tell me you're joking, for heaven's sake!'

'Keep your voice down, mate,' Joe advised, moving Simpson a little away from a couple of burly labouring types who had turned round with an unfriendly stare. 'There's alcohol in the things, same as in the beer-cakes. I don't know how they do it, but they do. You'll see. Come on, what about another? Forget our sorrows.'

'My turn,' Simpson said. 'No, Ernie, let me, I'd like to.'

'How are you for cash?'

Simpson produced his wallet, which was stuffed with pound notes unimprovably forged by our Temporal Treasury. 'That ought to be enough, oughtn't it?'

'Fine, but have you got change? Thirty pence a pint, it is.'

'Ninety altogether. I can give him a pound and get ten pence change.'

'Well . . . you can't, Simmy, sorry. Nobody gives change any more, except at the change shops. You got to have the exact money, because it's –'

'I know!' Simpson shrieked. This last, trivial revelation turned his mounting despair to fury. 'It's too much trouble! Too much trouble to hand over a coin! Too much bloody trouble! What's the matter with you all? Oh, you two are decent enough blokes, but you're spineless! You've given in to the system! You must fight it!'

He yelled more in the same strain, but could not afterwards remember just what. Indeed, the whole situation immediately became confused. He took a swingeing punch on the ear, probably from one of the labourers who had glared at him earlier, and staggered sideways into the throng away from Ernie and Joe, whom he saw no more. Further blows fell on him, accompanied by shouts of 'Student! Another bloody student! Let's do this one up proper!' The landlord arrived, not, it transpired, to separate the combatants, nor to throw Simpson out, but to join in beating him up.

Things were looking desperate, and Simpson was dimly relinquishing hopes of ever returning to 1975, when a new arrival, previously unseen, entered the fray on his side. With swift, well-aimed punches this person disposed of the immediate opposition and hauled Simpson out into the street. They ran. Guided by his rescuer, Simpson stumbled

into an alley and found himself pushed behind a fire-escape.
In the middle distance were sounds of a pursuit assembling.

'This is a cul-de-sac,' Simpson panted.

'That's why they won't look here yet,' the other man said,
breathing easily.

'God, you're in good trim. Back there, the way you –'

'I ought to be. I've had eight years to train for this.'

The voice was eerily familiar. So – Simpson studied it for
the first time – was the face. A little redder, hair a little
greyer, but . . .

'My God . . . it's you. I mean me.'

'If we stick to regarding each other as two different
persons, which we are, we'll get on better', Simpson II said,
with the authority of one who has everything thought out in
advance. 'We've got a moment's breather now. You'd
better use it.'

'But how do I get back?' Simpson asked wildly, ignoring
this advice.

'I'll show you. It's all lined up.'

'Why did they send you?'

'I was the only fit man on the team' (Simpson grinned at
each of us in turn when he reached this part of his story)
'and we didn't dare tell anyone else. I knew the exact
situation in the pub, too.'

'You took your time about coming.'

'Sorry. I had a long journey. And then there was traffic.
Big meeting in Trafalgar Square about legalizing heroin.'

A straggle of men calling for student blood ran in-
efficiently past the open end of the alley. When the sounds
had died away, Simpson II pulled Simpson out of cover and
led him across to a dilapidated and empty garage.

'In here. Quick. Put this in your pocket.'

'What is it?'

'Full report on the occupation of Mars.'

'But . . .' It took Simpson, flustered as he was, a moment
to remember what was his official reason for being there at
all. Then he recoiled. 'But I can't transfer something from

one time to another! They're always on about it, especially the Director. Danger of a paradox or a –'

Speaking with great emphasis, Simpson II swept this objection aside. (Simpson, now almost cheerful, insisted on reporting verbatim the terms in which he did so.) 'If you leave it behind you'll have failed in your mission so totally that you'll never get a decent job again. And you're going to need that for the money. And since I've lived through what's going to happen to you after this, I know you're going to have taken it with you, so get on with it and stop arguing.'

'All right. Thanks.'

'A pleasure.'

Simpson was about to depart when he remembered something vital, and turned. 'Hey, before I go – is the drink situation really quite hopeless?'

'Put it this way,' Simpson II said in a hurry: 'the 1981 El Minya whites are almost . . .'

He broke off abruptly as shouts and running footfalls came into earshot again. Propelled by his rescuer, Simpson half-fell through the garage doorway and at once the TIOPEPE grabbed him.

'El Minya,' the Director said. 'Somewhere in Spain, no doubt. Never heard of it. Anyway, the Spanish white wines are all terrible, aren't they? Still, I suppose when there's nothing else . . .'

'They'd be in wine-cakes like the rest of the stuff.' Simpson's earlier gloom had returned in full.

Rabaiotti said nothing. I said nothing. Schneider had slipped away, perhaps to fetch the drinks we so sorely needed.

'Well,' the Director said, trying to strike a consoling note, 'it's just a phase, isn't it? That's the way to look at it. After all, everything was all right again in 2010 when you went there, Simpson. And the position couldn't have cured itself in a couple of months.'

'No, it might take twenty years. That's 1990. Say ten of those twenty years to get things back into reasonable shape. That's 2000. Say the 1983 situation had only been going in full for three years, which is pretty bloody optimistic. That's 1980. So from then until 2000 or so it'll be wine-cakes and beer-cakes. Oh, it'll look like a phase from 2050 all right. But what good's that?'

'There's spirits,' Rabaiotti muttered.

'I didn't taste those. I expect they'll make you drunk, though. Which is how I intend to be for the duration of the phase.'

The others nodded hopelessly. Then Schneider came tearing back into the lab, a large book held open in front of him.

'El Minya!' he screeched. 'El Minya!'

In a moment we were clustered round him. 'What is it? What have you – ?'

'I knew I knew it! It was one of the German objectives in 1943. It's not in Spain, it's in Egypt. On the Nile. Here, look at the atlas. Don't you see? Israel! The only place where that Ernie chap said things were different!'

'But Israel only goes up to the Suez Canal in that part' I objected.

'Now it does! *Now* it does! Just the other day there was a report that they were preparing to get on the march again. The finest agriculturalists in the world! Who can make the desert blossom like a rose! Or flourish like a vine!'

The Director looked round the circle, beaming. 'Saved, gentlemen! No wonder you, Simpson, or rather the other you, said you'd had a long journey. All the way from Jerusalem!'

Kingsley Amis

Dear Illusion

'He is good, is he?' asked Pat Bowes, turning the car out of the main shopping street of the town into a lane that gave a glimpse of distant greenery. 'I mean I know people go on about him, but who don't they go on about these days? But he's supposed to be good in the same way as, I don't know, Keats and Milton and Christ, you'll have to help me out, not Shakespeare, Gerald Manley Hopkins. Isn't he?'

'How do you know about Hopkins?'

'I did him at school. I thought he came on a bit strong myself; you know, working himself up over not a hell of a lot. But the master was all for him. Great genius type of thing. I hope this is right.'

'First left after the bridge.' Sue Macnamara glanced at the typewritten sheet with the name of a national newspaper at the head of it. 'Wind-pump on the left – that must be that thing. Then left again after two hundred yards. Yes, Milton would be putting him a bit too high, but he's up with Keats and Hopkins all right, or so they say.'

'So they say was what I said. What do you say yourself?'

'I don't say anything much. I don't know.'

'But that's the sort of thing you're paid to know, Macnamara. This must be the turning. You with a degree from Cambridge College and all.'

'The works of Edward Arthur Potter weren't in my syllabus, Bowes. Anyway, one big thing about those works is that they're damned difficult. I was brought up on stuff you could make a bit of head or tail of. I suspect Potter of not being as good as he looks or sounds, but only suspect. And the critics are no help. They nearly all think he's great, but then they nearly all think people I know are bloody awful are great too. Here we are.'

'Edward Arthur Potter.' Bowes pulled up the estate wagon outside a longish, low house of pale stone. 'That's a crappy name. Ted Potter's what he's called. Like that composer bloke, Richard Robert Rodney Robin Roger Ronald Rooney Bennett. He means Dick Bennett. You go and knock on the door while I start shifting the gear.'

Sue Macnamara, a long-legged girl of thirty, got down and opened a creaking iron gate in the middle of a fence made of tall loops of iron. There was strong July sunlight, a smell of already rotten fruit and the droning of unseen but what sounded like oversized insects. Nothing had been done about the grass and other vegetation in the short front garden for quite a time. Like the window-frames, the front door was painted a shade of light blue that somebody must have noticed a long way from this or any other part of Kent and decided was appropriate to a poet's cottage. It – the front door – opened before it could be knocked on and a little old man appeared.

'Miss Macnamara?'

'Mrs. Sorry, I should have . . . You must be Mr Potter.'

She spoke without conviction. The face that looked hard but rather uninterestedly into hers – largely a matter of silvery-rimmed glasses, broad pointed nose and deep under-lip, the whole squashed on to very little in the way of a neck – did almost nothing to evoke the two or three standard photographs of Edward Arthur Potter she was used to seeing. Not quite nothing, though: there was just about enough likeness to suggest some doddering uncle or remoter connection supported out of charity, even a half-brother born of a feeble-minded kitchen-maid near the end of the last century. But anyone like that would probably be called Potter too, Sue thought to herself without urgency, shaking a small thick hand and responding to a smile that showed a few widely-separated teeth.

'Yes. Yes, that's right.' The reply showed apparent surprise, as at a lucky hit. 'I thought the paper said you were bringing someone else with you, Mrs Macnamara. A photographer.'

He stressed the last word on its first and third syllables, giving it a downward social shove thereby, ranging it alongside piano-tuner and picture-framer. A handy one to use on Bowes when the moment came, thought Sue. She said,

'Yes, he's coming now. Fetching his stuff from the car.'

'So he is. It's these glasses. I can't seem to find the other pair. Not that they're much help. I must go and see the optician again.'

Bowes came bustling up the flagged path, hung about the shoulders with cameras and light-meters and clutching among other things a tripod of metallic tubing. With his squat body, round pale face and habitually open mouth, he looked to Sue as little competent to be a photographer, even in the degraded sense of one who photographed, as Edward Arthur Potter looked like a poet. She would have denied that she was one of those who expected a poet to look like an actor, or even like the kind of person the kind of actor that came to mind habitually acted: peasant revolutionary, dedicated scientist, early-Christian martyr. And she knew well enough that poets were not supposed to talk like actors, like actors when acting, at least. Nevertheless, this poet's total lack of physical poeticality was a let-down, along with his manner of speech: slow, faintly glutinous, and couched in a rustic cockney that got the worst of two semi-separable worlds. Sue missed the touch of the charlatan that, after six years of this sort of journalism for the papers and television, she had learnt to expect in people who had to any degree deserved their success: not counting actors and actresses, of course, who behaved like charlatans whether they were any good or not.

Some of this occurred to her later; for the moment, all was action of a limited sort. Introductions were made, and Bowes at once ordered Potter out of his own house into its back garden. He did this in a way that showed he thought he knew just how to get people to do what he wanted without their ever feeling any pressure. In the garden, or the fenced-off bit of field where nothing grew but grass, two or three fruit-trees well past the arboreal change of life and a few clumps of tattered dandelions, he started moving pieces of outdoor furniture and other objects about with a photographer's unconsidering roughness, not out of any apparent impatience but as if all private property not his own were public property. Sue used this (as it proved) considerable intermission to show what was a genuine acquaintance with some of Potter's work, mentioning a couple of individual poems. Potter showed mild and unfeigned surprise.

'I didn't think anybody really read me these days. Nobody under about sixty, anyway. When did you first come across "Drizzle and Thrush"?'

'When it first appeared. In the *New Statesman*, wasn't it?'

'Not just homework, then. Mind you, I'm all for homework. Did you like it?'

'I'm not sure.' Sue discarded without forethought the lying flattery she had been ready with.

'Neither am I, my dear, neither am I. That's the problem. My problem, I should say. Would you like some tea or something?'

'Not for me, thank you,' she said, wanting to avoid a second bout of delay before the interview could start. Then she caught a mental glimpse of an apple-cheeked, check-aproned wife buttering home-made scones in the kitchen. 'But if you and Mrs Potter were thinking of...'

'She's not here. My wife's... not here.'

He spoke with great but unspecific force, implying anything from violent death to a grossly whimsical sortie round the shops in the town. Sue, whose thorough self-briefing had indicated a Mrs Potter alive and in residence, responded with a dead bat.

'You're on your own for a little while, then.'

'Yes, I am, and a very unpleasant mode of existence it is too, I don't mind telling you. I avoid it whenever I can. But the woman who looks after my sister-in-law, who can't move, fell downstairs on Monday and broke both her legs, so I've had to let my wife go until such time as they can find someone else. That's why I'm glad you don't want any tea, because I'd have had to go and get it. In my experience, no kind of meal or refreshment is worth a single moment's preparation. On one's own part, that is.'

'What do you live on, then, when Mrs Potter's away?'

'Beer and cornflakes mostly. I don't take sugar on them, the cornflakes, so that's one bit of bother saved. Of course, there is opening the new packet. I can't see any way round that.'

Neither could Sue, but she was saved having to admit as much by the intervention of Bowes, who sat Potter down in one of Potter's garden chairs, a canvas-and-rusted-metal affair, in the manner of an army dentist with a battalion's worth of extractions and fillings before him. His thrusting of a light-meter to within an inch of Potter's face was also faintly dental, suggesting a dry run with syringe or drill-head. Sue found herself stationed in a similar chair near Potter at one of the comparatively few angles nobody would naturally choose for any sort of conversation. Not far off, Bowes had thrown together a sort of cairn of stuff he must have found lying about: a couple of metal drums that might once have held paraffin, some cardboard boxes, some flower-pots, some white-painted rocks fit for a past or future rock-garden, a primordial lawn-mower, a half-sized St Francis or related figure in dirty stone. Without any trouble, Sue could visualize the end-product of this arrangement as a fashionable back-to-front portrait, a sprawling, blurred mélange in the foreground with the tiny in-focus shape of

Potter in the distance, plus, no doubt, about two fifths of herself at the edge – whatever fraction would most bore and annoy the beholder. Right up the art editor's street, and Bowes would know it; but he was not the sort of photographer, nor the sort of man, to have two or three tries at something when two or three hundred would do. Here he was in his ritual dance, approaching, retreating, squatting, on tiptoe, clicking, winding on, now and then standing stockstill to gaze at Potter in evident consternation, only to go twitching back into the measure.

Sue had opened her notepad. 'Before we begin, Mr Potter, I should tell you that you'll be sent a proof of the article in advance, so that you can make any alterations or cuts.'

'I say, that's jolly decent of you. Not many of you do that.'

'I think quite a lot of people are more forthcoming if they know they have that sort of control.'

'Enlightened self-interest, which is very enlightened. Right, then. I was born in Croydon, Surrey, in 1899, and educated at the –'

'Excuse me, Mr Potter: I think I already have really all the obvious known facts about you, what with the Lacey-Jones book, and your publisher . . .'

'Good Lord.' He lifted his glasses above his eyebrows and looked at her as hard as he had done when they first met, but this time not uninterestedly. His eyes were light brown, with darker flecks, 'This is the first time one of you has ever . . . But then you're not really one of you, if I make myself clear. I should have seen that before.'

'Could we have the glasses up again, please?' said Bowes in a managerial tone, and fell to bobbing and straightening as he clicked his way round a semi-circle that brought his camera within a hand's breadth of Sue's ear. She said to Potter, who was still obediently holding his glasses up in the required position,

'Can you think while this sort of thing's going on?'

'I can think while any sort of thing's going on, in so far as I can think at all. I wrote my first poems while I was working in a timber yard. But you'll have read about all that. What there was of that, I mean.'

'Can I ask you about those first poems? And about what made you write them? I'm sorry, I know that's a damned silly question, but our readership's not of a very –'

'I think it's a fascinating question, not as regards me personally, but as regards all writers of poems. But before we get on to it, I'll save you the embarrassment of asking another question I'm sure you'll quite reasonably want to ask. I write with a pen or a pencil, or anything that makes marks, on any sort of paper. I expect if I had nothing but a blackboard and a piece of chalk I could manage with them. Not a typewriter: I've nothing against the typewriter, I just can't use it, not even for the fair copies – I get my wife to do them, and then she sends them off to my agent without my looking at them again. She keeps a carbon for the files. She does all that, very nicely too.'

'I see. Why don't you look at the fair copies before they go off?'

'No point in it. I write very clearly and my wife's a very accurate typist.'

'So in a sense the first you see of the poem in its finished state is when it appears in print.'

Potter glanced over at Bowes, who was doing something technical to one of his cameras, or trying to. 'Well ... it'd be truer to say that the last I see of it in its finished state is when I give the manuscript of it to my wife for her to type it out.'

'You mean you don't ever ... you don't normally look at it when it's originally published? I suppose it is more satisfying to wait until you've got a whole collection in front of you, inside hard covers, properly done. The way they lay poems out in magazines and so on is often very ... shoddy ...'

'Some – some people probably do find a book of things

they've written more satisfying than the separate bits typed out or in a magazine. I just find it more frightening.'

'Frightening?' Sue was nearly certain that Potter had never publicly talked to this effect before, but the rising excitement she felt (and tried to conceal) was more than journalistic. 'Why do you say that?'

'Seven books of my poems have been published, and they all cover, each one covers about five years' work. Seven fives are thirty-five: I started late. As you know, Mrs Macnamara, but that's by the way. One book is five years' work, and five years' work is roughly between fifty and sixty poems, and that's all. What I mean by that is that that's all I do in the five years that I count as doing anything. I worked in the timber yard and then in that factory office, and afterwards for those tinned-fruit people until I'd started making enough money from my poems to retire. As you know. It was work, at the timber yard and the other places: somebody had to do it and I'm not despising it: but I don't count it. All I count is the books, and unless the books – '

'We'll take the break there,' said Bowes generously, coming down to a stooped position at the mid-point of the triangle formed by Potter, Sue and the heap of properties. 'Very good, both of you. Now you relax while I go and reload and do a bit of minor surgery on this bit of Jap iron-mongery' – he waved an offending camera – 'out in the car. Rejoin us in a couple of minutes.'

When he had gone, Sue lit a cigarette and considered, as calmly as possible, how to lead Potter back and round and along and forward again to the point he had reached when interrupted. 'Could you tell me a little more about how you write? How a poem takes shape, or how you know when it has?'

'Lots of words and phrases go through a person's mind all the time without staying there. At least they do through mine. Then, every so often, without the person knowing why, one of the words or phrases, it just sticks there and won't go away. That's the beginning. I don't mean necessarily the beginning of the poem when you see it when you read it, but it can be, quite often it is, but it's your way into the poem, if that doesn't sound too silly. I mean it's the man who's writing the poem's way into his poem. Then a lot more words go on going through until another one gets caught, like in a net, and it sticks with the first ones because it belongs with them, you realize, or you realize later that it belongs with them. And so on. Do you fuck?'

'Yes, but only my husband,' said Sue with fair approximation to the truth.

'That's a pity. I mean it's a pity for me, because I get so few chances these days: I can quite see it's a jolly good thing for you. And your husband. I'm in the same sort of position myself as a rule, but obviously a good deal less so, if that makes any sense, because I don't happen to be very attracted to women of sixty-eight. That's how old my wife is, you see. With her being away, and you being here anyhow, so to speak, I thought it would be silly not to just ask. And then in the end it dawns on you that there's no more to come, not this time, that's all there's going to be of it. The thing's over and done with and finished. At that point you write it down.'

It was not until now that Sue realized that, for the past quarter of a minute, Potter had been talking about his poetry again. His question had taken her completely by surprise, a gigantic achievement in the face of one so constantly asked if she fucked (in those or other terms) as Sue Macnamara: no preliminary switching-on of casualness, no quick range-estimating glance, no perceptible inner shaping up or squaring of the shoulders, nothing. In the same way, her refusal had evoked not the least hint of pique, mortification, retrospective embarrassment or – what she had noticed as quite common among the over-fifties – ill-dissimulated relief: all this gathered up in his not having bothered to make anything whatever in the way of an as-I-was-saying gesture before he went back to his previous theme, about which something had better be said soon on her own part.

'I see. You always wait until the poem's complete in your mind before you put anything on paper.'

'Normally. If I've got to go and get on a train or something like that before it's finished, I write down as much as I've done and then think about something else until I can have another go at it. That seems to work.'

'Sorry about that,' said Bowes as he approached, expressing sincere regret for having, however unavoidably, let the rest of the company in for a stretch of utter idleness. He went into a prowling circuit of the space where they sat, every few steps snatching his camera up to eye-level, failing to take a photograph and subsiding again: a more intrusive routine, if anything, than the clicking and buzzing it replaced. But at least he was about, and so might deter Potter from asking Sue just how it had come to pass that she only fucked her husband, should it occur to Potter to do so.

'When the poem's all there on paper, do you revise it much?'

'Not at all, ever. I don't even read it through. I give it straight to my wife to type, or if it's the middle of the night I leave it face down on my table until I can give it to her.'

'You were saying you didn't read it, any given poem, when it's typed or even when it comes out in a magazine. When do you read it?'

Potter moved the tip of his tongue to and fro between gaps in his teeth. 'I suppose I must have read all my poems at least once. But it's not a thing I dwell on, or enjoy at all. The early morning's the only time. Then I may pick up one of my books and read a few things. To remind myself I've done them, more than anything else. I keep a count of how many I've done. I've just finished number four hundred and twenty-three. I wrote it out just this morning, as a matter of fact.'

'What do you feel when you read one of your poems?'

'If I'm lucky, relief that it doesn't seem any worse than it seems. Often, I wonder what on earth I meant, but I don't try to remember. Or it just doesn't register in any way.'

'No pleasure? Pride in achievement?'

'Achievement? No, nothing like that.'

Having learnt how easily a revelation of real interest could stem the most torrential flow of confidences or confessions, Sue tried to keep up her bright, nurse-like tone. 'Another over-simplifying question, I'm afraid, Mr Potter: why do you write poetry?'

'No, I think it really is a simple question. Or perhaps I just mean the answer I personally would give's quite simple. I write poetry to be able to go on living at all. Well, not quite at all, but to function as a human being. I'm afraid that doesn't sound very simple now I've said it. I'll have to risk you putting me down as pompous and sorry for myself. When I was working in that timber yard, my life started being a burden to me. Not just the life in the yard, but the whole of my life. It happened quite suddenly and I'll never know why. Nothing had gone wrong; I was happily married, in a secure job and earning enough to keep the two of us in reasonable comfort – we've never had the luck to have any children, but it wasn't that either. I stopped being able to enjoy anything or see the point of anything. I felt bad from morning to night every day. Then, after about a month, some words came into my mind and straight away I felt a little better. I forget what they were, but they brought more words with them and they made me feel a little better still. By the time the words stopped coming I felt at peace. I wrote them down on the back of a delivery note – I do remember that – and it was only then I woke up to the fact that what I'd done was write a poem. The moment I'd finished writing the words down I started feeling bad again. Not as bad as just before the words started coming, but still bad. The next day I felt a little worse, and the day after that worse again, and so on for another three or four weeks until another lot of words started turning up. It's been like that ever since.'

'This feeling bad,' said Sue, telling herself that after all she was a journalist – 'can you describe it any more fully?'

'No. If I could I would, believe me. I don't know what the poems have to do with it, either. I tried once not writing the poem down, but all that happened then was that I forgot it and started feeling bad again, so the only net result was that I was a poem short. Of course, if you look at it in one way, it's all rather like that business they call occupational therapy, where people weave carpets to take their mind off themselves and their problems. The point there is that it doesn't make any difference to anybody whether the carpets are any good or not. I've been wondering for over thirty years, on and off, if it's the same with my poems.'

The placid, rather monotonous voice stopped as Bowes shoved his stocky bulk squarely between the other two and let off a long burst of click-and-buzz. He had been well within earshot for some time, but his assumption of his own total primacy over anybody interviewing or being interviewed had its helpful side: he was stone-deaf to all talk not directly about sex, cars or photography. Sue thought Potter might have guessed something of the sort. She used the couple of minutes' interval to complete, in her own semi-shorthand, a nearly verbatim account of what Potter had said in the last four or five. She was certain that the information in it had never been divulged before.

Clearly and succinctly, Bowes now intimated that they were all to move indoors, to where Potter worked. Potter said he worked nowhere in particular, or everywhere, though there was a little table where he occasionally wrote things down, and Bowes answered that that was what he had meant.

They entered a low-ceilinged room that quite a few people would have felt inclined to call a parlour. By a window giving on to the front garden there was a characterless table and a hard chair with a flattened cushion. On the table Sue saw a cheap scribbling pad, one of its sheets detached and showing evidence of writing on the side not in view: no doubt that morning's poem. Bowes at once set about assembling an indoor cairn on a larger, oval table: a biscuit-barrel and two empty decanters from the sideboard, ornamental mugs and pottery figures from the mantelshelf, a multi-tiered cake-stand complete. The general style of these, and of other objects in the room, was in a current fashion, but that would be coincidence; they must be survivals of what the Potters had bought when they were first married in 1924, or had come by from their parents. To judge from his behaviour, and the shakier evidence of his work, Potter was not a man to care for or notice what was around him.

Sue moved to a small bookcase that held the expected complete works in the expected new-looking condition, and a few dozen other volumes, mostly paperbacked and all, or all of those she could take in at a glance, by authors she had never heard of. Potter's reading habits were well enough known, but she judged that a short trot over familiar ground would give him time to adjust to the change of scene and, with luck, to prepare himself for further revelations.

'Do you read a lot, Mr Potter?' asked Sue, while Bowes began setting up his lights and reflectors.

'Not a lot, no. I've never really taken to it. Either it's in you or it isn't is how I'd put it, and it doesn't seem to be in me. Oh, I quite enjoy books about Poland and Samoa and places like that where I've never been, but that's about as far as it goes.'

'No poetry?'

'Yes, a little from time to time, just to see what other people are doing. I sometimes buy one of those anthologies.'

'Who do you like particularly?'

'Well, it's hard to say. The standard seems to be so high, it's amazing. Let's see, I like Christopher Logue, John Betjeman, Allen Ginsberg, Philip Roth, Basil Bunting, John Berryman, Roy Fuller, John Lennon, Sylvia Plath, Fats Larwood, Robert Lowell ... And Ezra Pound and W. H. Auden, of course. But, as I say, so many people are good.'

'But surely –' Sue cut herself off, realizing she could not say any of the seven or eight things she wanted to say. 'Surely you prefer some of those names to others?'

'Not . . . not really.'

'I see. Have you any, what our readers would call hobbies?'

'You mean how do I spend my time. I do quite a lot of walking; there's still some country left round here. I have to answer quite a few letters, and then my agent rings me up. And in the evenings my wife and I play halma or something, or we watch television.'

'In the chair, please, Mr Potter,' said Bowes opportunely, setting off the equivalent of a smallish, slow-burning phosphorus bomb. 'That's lovely. Doing very well.'

Potter sat on for a few moments, seeming to shrink a little physically in the glare. Then he said, 'As I was telling you, Mrs Macnamara, I keep wondering about those poems of mine. The people who weave those carpets have had other things in their lives. They've done other things. They've been builders or lawyers or sailors or mothers or lorry-drivers or something. Or they've told jokes very well or got drunk a lot or . . . had a lot of women or played tennis or travelled or helped other people. I couldn't have done some of those things and I didn't want to do any of the others. I've never done anything but write poems. So if the poems are no good my life's been wasted.'

'Oh, but everybody agrees they're good. I was reading –'

'Not everybody. I don't agree for one. I don't say I disagree, but I don't agree. And unless I'm very much mistaken, neither do you.'

Sue could find nothing to say. She flinched at a sudden click-accompanied movement of Bowes behind her shoulder.

'Good.' Potter nodded approvingly. 'Well, my dear, I was afraid all that was going to sound pompous, and it has. And not only sounded pompous. I think I must have got more conceited as I've grown older. It's conceited of me to wonder whether I'm anything more than somebody who's been lucky enough to be able to make up his own occupational therapy without any help from outside. But it's a bad bargain no matter how you look at it.'

'Could I have you writing, please?' ordered Bowes from the shadows.

'Of course,' said Potter, taking out a felt-tipped pen and doodling quite convincingly on his pad. 'It's a bad bargain even if the poems are good. Whatever that may mean. From my point of view, nothing at all could compensate for getting on for forty years of feeling bad with a couple of days of not feeling so bad and ten minutes of feeling all right thrown in about once a month. There's a very good young doctor in the town here who took over not so long ago from the fellow I've always had. He reads a bit of poetry and he says he likes what I write. I've told him a lot of what I've told you. He takes my point about occupational therapy and he says I sort of psychoanalyse myself through my work so that I can carry on. But I'm fed up with carrying on. He's got every pill under the sun in that surgery of his, and he says he could probably find one that would make me feel all right most of the time, but it would probably, at least as probably, stop me wanting to write poems, or having to write poems. I've been holding out against that for about six months. Conceit again, I suppose. But I've decided I'm too old to be conceited any more. I'd like to feel all right for the rest of my life and never mind the poetry. So I'm stopping it, the poetry. In fact I have stopped. This one this morning was the last. Tomorrow morning I'll be off to see that doctor and he'll start me on what he calls a course. I'm really quite excited about it.'

'Now I'd like you looking as if you're looking for inspiration,' said Bowes.

Potter raised his head and eyes to the ceiling less like a looker for inspiration than a man inwardly calling for celestial vengeance on some other party.

'Can I print that?' Sue recognized that the question

she had been trying to frame, about why she was being told all this, had been answered. 'About your giving up poetry?'

'Oh, certainly. After all, this is an interview.'

'You realize it's news?'

'News? Well, some very funny things seem to be news these days, don't they? Do you want to telephone your editor?'

'No thank you,' she said, having, as he spoke, faced and solved a dilemma: whether to approach as soon as possible the parent newspaper for whose colour magazine she regularly wrote and had come here today, or to say nothing and allow her report of the interview, adorned with Bowes's efforts, to appear as planned in (perhaps) four months' time. If Potter told his piece of news to the representative of some other journal in the meanwhile, a lot of people would be cross with her, and her article, with its climactic point already common knowledge, might suffer severe cuts or even not appear at all. But that was just as likely to be its fate if she took the first of the two courses open to her, and she recoiled from the prospect of seeing an abbreviated, garbled and vulgarized version of her material under some such heading as 'Veteran Bard Lays Down Pen'. It must be the second alternative, then, with the comforting thought that, since nobody on the magazine was inquisitive enough to read copy on the look-out for possible news items, or indeed for almost any other reason, the laying-down of the pen might very well rest securely in its context until her publication day.

'Is there going to be much more of this?' asked Potter, who was still looking, in fact glaring by now, high over Sue's head. 'I'm afraid I find it rather tiring.'

'How many more, Pat?'

'Nearly there. Another couple.'

That meant a dozen or so, but a quick dozen. For the second time in five minutes, Sue searched for a remark. Finally she said,

'You must think of the thousands and thousands of people whom you've given pleasure.'

'Yes, I do try to sometimes. It's true I get a lot of letters saying some very nice things, and believe me I'm not at all ungrateful, but –'

'Could you relax and look out of the window as if you're thinking?'

'I'll do my best,' said Potter, setting a new lower limit to the amount of dryness the tone of a human voice could carry without its being altogether imperceptible. 'But, as I was going to say, I have wondered if the pleasure people say I've given them mightn't have prevented them from coming by some much higher kind of pleasure from other writers of poetry who really are good. I expect all this pop music prevents some youngsters from ever appreciating Brahms or Elgar.'

'You must know that's not a fair comparison, Mr Potter. And I don't think it's true anyway, your example.'

'Perhaps it isn't, my example. There's no way of knowing.'

'Right, that's it,' said Bowes. 'I've got some first-class ones there. Thank you for being so patient, Mr Potter. I can tell you're a pro at this job.'

The lights went and for a second or two the room seemed dark; then Sue saw it was only late afternoon outside. Bowes started disassembling his equipment while Potter, on his feet, stuck his hands in his pockets and stared at the floor. Sue waited until Bowes had gone out to the car and then said,

'I don't want to poke my nose in, but what are you having for your dinner tonight?'

'Cornflakes and a couple of sardines, I thought. And a bottle of light ale.'

'But that's not enough. You must have a proper meal. Something hot.'

'I can't be bothered.'

'May I see your kitchen?'

37

'Yes, it's just . . . through the . . . in here.'

In one corner of the small room was a tiny larder containing a good deal of tinned and cartoned food and very little fresh food. Sue made a selection from the tins, found two Spanish onions that seemed to have started to lose weight, decided that some cold boiled potatoes must be harmless despite their appearance, and looked round for a frying-pan.

'What are you doing?' asked Potter as if the preparation of a meal were genuinely strange and wonderful to him.

'Do you like corned-beef hash?'

'I like all food, but I don't see –'

'I'll just have a word with Mr Bowes.'

The word, or words, told Bowes that Potter wanted to add some information in total confidence. Tractable as ever outside the photographic sphere, Bowes at once said he would go and have a pint at a pub he had noticed a couple of hundred yards back down the road, and that Sue could join him there at any time she might fancy.

Back in the kitchen, Sue found Potter standing, presumably by chance, exactly beneath a well-patronized fly-paper that hung from the ceiling. He said,

'I don't want you to go to any trouble on my account.'

'It's very little trouble.' She set about peeling and slicing the onions. 'It's a small return for all the help you've given Mr Bowes and me. Now I'm going to cook this to the point where all you have to do is warm it up before you eat it. Can I trust you to do that?'

'Yes. Yes, I'll do that.'

Nothing more was said for some minutes, while she went on with her work. Then he asked abruptly,

'Would you consider staying on here a little while and sharing the corned-beef hash with me?'

'I'd like to, Mr Potter, but I'm afraid I've –'

'No, of course, yes, I quite see.'

The immediacy of his interruption showed her in the plainest terms that he had taken her to be simply blocking off the possibility of a return to the question he had put to her in the garden. She turned away from the gas stove, went over and took him by the hand.

'I shall have to go quite soon, Mr Potter,' she said slowly, 'because I have to be back in London in time for my husband to take me to the theatre. Do you see now?'

He nodded, not perfunctorily, and moved towards the window. She worked on through another pause, which again he broke.

'Mrs Macnamara, I want to ask you a fact, but you must understand I need it just as a fact, nothing more. What's your Christian name?'

'Susan, but I'm always called Sue.'

'Is that s, u, e?'

'Yes.'

'Thank you.'

He left the room and stayed away until the hash was nearly ready. When he came back he was carrying a sheet, now folded in two, of the paper she had seen on his table.

'I think you'll know what this is, Mrs Macnamara. I'd like you to accept it as a very small mark of my esteem, and as a way of saying thank you for being so sympathetic and understanding.' (A careful rehearsal of this in the parlour was not very difficult to imagine.) 'Please don't look at it until you've left here,' he went on, holding the paper out to her. 'There are no surprises, but I'd just rather you didn't.'

'You've made a copy of it, have you?'

'No. I never do that.'

'But what about your wife typing it out? I can't walk away with a unique copy. Suppose I lost it? And what about publication?'

'I don't suppose you'll lose it. If you really want to, perhaps you could type it out one day and send a copy to my agent' – whom he named – 'and a carbon here. Addressed to my wife. Please take it.'

She took the sheet, faintly warm from his hand. 'I don't know what to say.'

'There's nothing that needs to be said. I've thanked you with that and you've thanked me by making me this splendid meal. Is it done? How do I heat it up?'

'Ten minutes on a half gas'll be enough.'

'Just as it is. I see. Now I mustn't keep you from your husband; I expect you're late already. Where's that young man got to?'

'He's waiting in the pub.'

'Good, so you'll be able to get back to London all right. It's been a great pleasure meeting you, Mrs Macnamara. Good-bye.'

'Good-bye, Mr Potter,' she said as they shook hands on the doorstep.

At the gate she looked back, but the door had already shut. Four telegraph poles away in the direction of the town Bowes's car was parked by an inn-sign. She began to walk slowly down the road towards it, wishing she had been able to think of some leave-taking message to Potter that would not have been either sickly or stilted, deciding to write him a letter the next day, then taking the sheet of paper from her handbag and unfolding it. The writing was in soft pencil, clear and commonplace. It read,

UNBORN

From summer evenings, gazing
heartrise always ahead, there,
book and dream,
                    reaching out,
ten miles of fields of raw daffodils
streets engines advertisement hoardings
all raw,
          myself raw,
                    but certain.

Swept now, swept
                    book
                    dream
                    field
                    street

> engines cheerfully off or rusted
> hoardings ablaze or demolished
> nobody there
>   Not unfound,
> not unreached, unborn
>   unfated.
>
> Dear illusion with the bright hair
> all swept aired lit plain known listed
>
> swept

At the foot were a couple of lines in the same hand, written upside down. She turned the sheet round and read,

> To Sue Macnamara with the kindest regards possible
>   from Ted Potter

That last was the product of something like ten minutes' thought, she said to herself, and written upside down to avert the risk of reading a single word of the poem.

2

The poem stayed in Sue's mind for the rest of the evening and, though diminishingly, much longer, both as a poem and as an amalgam of less clearly definable things: a piece of self-revelation that might fall anywhere between compressed but pondered autobiography and record of a passing mood, a gift to herself offered out of considered or unconsidered politeness, desire to return a favour that might or might not have seemed unimportant. Typing it out next morning inevitably forced her to read it as a poem a good deal more closely than (she admitted to herself) she had ever read a Potter poem before.

It was probably this closeness that made its theme effortlessly plain to her – and this, in turn, suggested an unpalatable reason for Potter's success with critics and public: he wrote in a way that looked and felt modern, or at any rate post-Georgian, but with a certain amount of effort could be paraphrased into something quite innocuously traditional, even romantic. And the reader's self-satisfaction at having made his way through apparent obscurity could easily be transmuted into affection for poem and poet.

In 'Unborn', at any rate, Potter, or some version of Potter, was just saying that an ideal he had pursued since youth had turned out to be not unrealized but unrealizable, because its object had never existed. What that object might have seemed to be was less plain: 'dear' along with 'bright hair' certainly suggested a woman – or a man, though nothing in his other works, or in gossip, or in what she had seen of him bore out that interpretation, which she discarded promptly and for good. But then, the brief and unspecific image of the 'dear illusion' might so easily refer not to a person at all, but to some abstraction dimly seen as a person, and almost any abstraction of the nicer sort would fit: love, happiness, beauty, joy, adventure, self-respect, self-mastery, self-sufficiency, God . . .

With the typing done and checked against the original, Sue knew 'Unborn' well, and the knowledge was, again, unpalatable. For a moment she felt cross with it: taken out of its drunkard's or dotard's telegraphese and put into plain English, conventionally assembled instead of sprawling hither and thither over the page, it would have shown itself up, she suspected, as being not only traditional but trite. And in what sense might (or could) the daffodils be raw? And were the hoardings ablaze with colour or literally on fire? And were there not too many '–ings' in the first half-dozen lines, and had 'hair' been intended to rhyme with 'there' in an otherwise rhymeless poem, and however that might be was it anything better than slack to let 'aired' in so soon afterwards? And '*heart*rise' (what a word, anyway) taken with '*ahead*' was somehow . . . Was just the sort of thing poets got rid of in revision.

Sue felt bad about raising these objections, even though she would always keep them to herself, which made it odder that the nearest imaginable comparison to how she felt was, it turned out, how she would feel if she were to show up a child's ignorance publicly. Had Potter not given her the manuscript there would have been no issue, but he had, and she had met him and listened to him, and so the poem took on the quality of a friend's muffled cry of distress without, unfortunately, ceasing to be a poem in its own right and demanding to be read as one. The only course was to try to forget its text while remembering its existence. She locked it away in a desk drawer among other keepsakes, wrote covering letters to go with the copies for Potter's agent and Mrs Potter, and then settled down to write to Potter himself. This final task proved less disagreeable than she had feared: she was thankful to be able to say with truth that she had been moved both by the gift and by reading what she had been given.

The following month, she sent Potter a proof of her piece. It came back unamended with a short handwritten note complimenting her on her accuracy – 'though you make me sound more clear-headed than I am sure I can have been' – and adding that the corned-beef hash had been delicious. About the same time, 'Unborn' was published in the *Listener*; she did not read it. After several more months, more than she had been led to expect in the first place but fewer than she had in fact expected, the magazine printed her article; she did not read that either, merely scanning it for cuts and mutilations, a virtually separate activity in somebody of her experience. There were, for once, no cuts. Bowes had, as always, produced pictures that were technically excellent and artistically sub-modish, though there was one indoor shot of Potter at his table that recalled him sharply: well enough, anyhow, for the fuzzy-edged bulk of an Edwardian tea-caddy, looming in the extreme foreground, to seem no worse than irrelevant. The news – it was news, since he had revealed nothing of it in the interim – the news of Potter's decision to put away his pen drew no public attention at the time. Those to whom it might have seemed important either ignored the interview altogether or failed

Kingsley Amis

to extricate such a disclosure from its context of travel
advertisements and illustrated recipes.

Something else Sue omitted to read, or to re-read, during
this period was any of Potter's other poems. She shied away
from the strong possibility of finding that she felt as uneasy
about them as she had about 'Unborn'. In the winter, the
magazine sent her to South America to do a series on what
it called the cultural life of the chief cities there. With her
went not Bowes, but a photographer of the alternative
sort, the sort that took at most one photograph of every
subject, and she slept with him a certain amount. Potter
began to fade from her mind. Then, almost exactly a year
after she had been to see him, she came across his name in an
arts-page headline in a Sunday paper.

Edward Arthur Potter (she read), who according to
rumour (in plain language, according to an authentic statement in another journal, she thought to herself) had taken a
vow of poetic silence, must have gone back on it, for his
publishers were to bring out in the coming autumn a
collection of his recent verse. There seemed to be hopes of
some commemorative event – an official dinner, an award –
that might go a little way to offset the shameful lack of
attention so far paid a man described as arguably Britain's
greatest living bard. The report closed with a passage of
largely directionless rancour about the neglect of Potter in
particular and almost everybody else in general.

The news pleased and worried Sue. Potter deserved
recognition as a – well, at least as someone who had devoted
the better part of his life to writing poetry, even if, or even
though, recognition of the sort in view might not appeal to
him much. On the other hand, it did seem very likely that
the pills from the hand of the young doctor had failed to do
their job, that Potter was back on his self-administered
version of occupational therapy and that he was again
spending nearly all his time feeling bad.

Worry about others' concerns, like pleasure on their
account, needs regular renewal if it is not to fall away; the

summer brought Sue fresh assignments and a falling-away of her worry and pleasure in the case of Potter's prospective award/dinner. But, in due time, award/dinner became award-dinner in a real sense. A body claiming, in its title, to superintend our culture announced that Edward Arthur Potter was shortly to receive a special prize of £1,000 to mark the publication of his latest book, *Off*, and to attest to his status as premier lyrist in the English language. The cheque, together with an ornamental certificate designed by a leading designer, would be handed over in the course of a function at a Regent Street restaurant famous until only a few years back for its food and service. A week after seeing this report, Sue got an invitation to the award-dinner. Stapled to a corner of the lavish card was a strip of flimsy which bore, in smudged carbon, a bald statement to the effect that this favour had come her way at Mr Potter's personal request – thus conveying, with masterly economy, the organizers' helplessness in the circumstances to prohibit the attendance of somebody they themselves would never have dreamt of asking along.

On the night, Sue left her husband contentedly watching television and appeared at the restaurant, the main bar of which turned out to be given over to the Potter occasion. She had arrived early, but there was already a fair-sized group round the man of the hour. Experience of such gatherings suggested her first move: getting one drink down her and another into her hand. There were plenty of recognizable faces, perhaps too many, not more than half of them belonging to the world of letters in even the most charitably extended sense of the phrase. A sports commentator, a girl who made boots, a television bishop in mufti, a man who not long before had covered half a mile of cliff near Dover with paint of various colours – all sorts of people who surely could not be famous just because of what they did, who did nothing else but what they did and who were famous all the same. Not only that: when she began her career, what had slightly astonished Sue at affairs of this sort was the number of old contemptibles, of those whose claim to fame, if any, dated so far into the past that they could more than safely be dropped. Tonight she was struck by the number and contemptibility of new contemptibles, persons categorically unfit (on all but the most trend-crazed reckoning) to be invited along to see Potter honoured. Thirty-three next year, she said to herself.

Having beaten off an embryonic pass by an elderly small boy who turned out to be a concrete poet, Sue made her way over to a couple of journalist acquaintances. The Press had come along all right. So had its visual auxiliaries: cameras flashed every few seconds. Somebody who ought to have been flashing away with the very, very best of them, but who did no more than drink and chat, was Pat Bowes, to whom Sue turned. He kissed her genially and said,

'You're looking smashing, Macnamara. Great lot here tonight, aren't they?'

'You look all right too, Bowes. Where's your camera?'

'At home. I'm here because I'm so distinguished, not to work. Mr Potter's personal request.'

'Me too. No notebook, thank God.'

'Nice of the old lad to ask me along. I mean it's obvious why he got hold of you, with you making that hit with him, but he needn't have asked me.'

'Well, you were nice to him the day we went there.'

'No I wasn't, love. I'm always a right bugger with my sitters, you know that. No, he asked me because he didn't like to think of me probably finding out you'd been here and thinking he hadn't bothered to remember me. I call that really nice.'

Sue nodded.

'What I don't understand is about this book. He told you he'd packed it all in. End of the road kind of style. He didn't strike me as the sort of bloke who'd change his mind about a thing as important to him as that.'

'Nor me. I don't know what's happened.'

'We won't find out tonight. The chances of a quiet confidential word with the guest of honour are, I would say, remote in the extreme. Not because of him – he'd much rather have a good natter with you than talk to all these important sods, but they've brought him here and they'll hang on to him. Anyway. Have the mag been on to you about Peduzzi?'

'No, what about him?'

'They will. Famed Macnamara-Bowes team spotlight yet another feature of the cultural scene. A pretty far-bloody-flung feature too. He's filming in Ceylon till the end of the month, they said, then a short stop-over in Italy before he takes off I forget where. I'd sooner do him in Ceylon myself, of course. Could you work it?'

'How long would it take?'

'I'd say five days minimum all in. He isn't sitting on his arse in Colombo, you see. There'd be ox-cart stuff before we could get to him.'

'I'll check and let you know.'

A vague plum-in-throat bawling emerged from the ambient uproar and resolved itself into, 'Mrs Macnamara, please. Mr Bowes, please.'

'Christ, we're being paged,' said Bowes. 'Butlered, rather.'

'Mr Potter,' said the functionary, looking from one to the other with open incredulity, 'would be obliged if you would join him for a few minutes.'

'Like two,' said Bowes to Sue as they followed. 'Or one and a half.'

Her first real look at Potter that evening showed a small neat dinner-jacketed figure without any of the soup-stains or shave-traces that might have been expected; she guessed the reason when she recognized his agent close to his side. There were a great many introductions, starting with the cultural bureaucrat in overall charge and the leading literary critic booked for the main speech – more leading, this one, than the leading designer of the certificate (who was also about the place) in the proportion of a knighthood

47

to an O.B.E. There would have been still more introductions if Potter had not cut them off by taking a long time over saying how glad he was to see Sue and Bowes again.

'Is Mrs Potter here this evening?' asked Sue.

'I'm afraid she's not in the best of health.'

'Sorry to hear that,' said Bowes.

Potter moved closer to Sue and said quietly, 'In fact there's absolutely nothing wrong with her. I just thought it would be better if she stayed away. You'll probably see what I mean by the time the evening's over. It's not her sort of thing at all.'

'No, well . . .'

'Have you seen my book yet, Mrs Macnamara? Have you, Mr Bowes? No, not a great many people have, outside the committee and so on. But there's a copy for everybody beside their place at dinner for them to take home, if they still want to after they've heard me speak. Anyway, I hope they give it a glance. I shall be most interested to hear what people think of it, more interested than with any of my previous books.'

There was a nervous jocularity in his tone and manner that Sue found mildly strange, until she noticed the glass of whisky in his hand and reflected that, for him, large parts of the evening would be an ordeal, and of an unfamiliar kind. Then he said to her, again in an undertone,

'Would you have a quick drink with me afterwards, Mrs Macnamara? Upstairs, in a little place called the Essex Room. I've spoken to one of these chaps about it. We'll be breaking up quite early.'

'Thank you, Mr Potter, I'd love to.'

'Good . . . Mr Bowes, I'm afraid I never thanked you for taking such magnificent photographs. I was going to write to you, but then I got bogged down with one thing and another, and then it seemed too late.'

'Don't worry about that. Glad you liked them.'

Here a Cabinet minister interposed himself between Sue and Potter, of whom she saw nothing further until the party, two hundred or more strong, was settling itself down at the couple of dozen large tables in the dining-room, a slow and lubberly process. Potter was among bureaucrats and critics and other poets and their wives halfway across the room from Sue. The first course, already in position, was pieces of tinned grapefruit apparently strung together on fine thread and adorned with a tattered cherry. She picked up the copy of *Off* that indeed lay by her plate and began, without eagerness, to glance through it.

The poems, she saw quite soon, did not really look like Potter poems, which, within wide limits, had always had a characteristic shape on the page, sprawling and staccato at the same time. The new ones did not much look like one another, either. From glancing through, she turned to reading. On an early page she found a piece in heroic couplets after the manner of Dryden – a long way after, she found, because it turned out to convey no meaning whatever at any point, could have been thrown off, dashed down as fast as his hand would travel over the paper by someone solely concerned with filling up iambic pentameters that rhymed. Beside it, 'Unborn' was a model of sober clarity. But 'Unborn' was not beside it, in the sense that it was not (she double-checked) in the book. Had it been one of a number of rejects, part of the whey thrown out when the cream was skimmed off for a new volume? In their interview, Potter had implied clearly that he reprinted in hard covers everything he wrote. Well, he might have omitted the poem in deference to a desire on his wife's part not to see the immortalization of that rival-figure, the bright charmer with the ... Sue tried to remember: dear charmer with the bright hair – no, not charmer. Dear something, though.

At this point she found that somebody had taken her grapefruit away and put some fish where it had been, while somebody else (probably) had poured her some wine. She tried to eat and easily succeeded in drinking. She also thought. This was made a little easier for her by her absorption until just now in *Off*: her neighbours' attention had been pre-empted by their further neighbours, and throughout the meal she got away with saying almost nothing, either to the disc-jockey on her left or to the plain, horse-oriented jockey on her right. From time to time she looked at *Off* again. One poem, or 'poem', she encountered ran,

Man through different shell all over turns into sea swelling birth
comes light through different man all over light shell into sea.
Rock waits noon out of sky by tree same turns into rock by noon out
of sky underneath tree out of same rock . Woman keeps flower beside
leaves every time towards fruited earth keeps leaves every time
towards flower fruited woman turns into earth beside leaves. Shell
all over man waits rock out of noon towards earth every time beside
woman. Man woman earth.

She found this about as digestible as the overcooked but lukewarm chicken *à la Kiev* that followed the fish. A glance over at Potter suggested that he was listening closely to whatever a bureaucrat or critic might have been telling him. Was he really listening, closely or not? Sue felt with uneasy certainty that there was something wrong or odd or out of place here. Where was here? In *Off*, to start with. For a final sample, she opened the book at its last page, and read,

> I slash the formless web of hate,
>   I plumb the worked-out mine of love;
> My wrist receives the birds that sate
>   Their lust engendered from above.
>
> While rosy sunsets lurch and fade
>   Across the endless strife of seed,
> The debt of living must be paid
>   To creditors who starve in need.

Whatever else that was or was not, it was not the voice of Potter as it had always been. Well, what of it? He was experimenting, looking for a new style; unusual and admirable at his time of life. Sue held on to that while the meal came to an end and the speeches got under way. The first of these began with a not very closely compressed account of the recent doings of the cultural body, retailed on a note of open and personal self-congratulation. Towards the end it bore round to the subject of poetry, and finally mentioned the name of Edward Arthur Potter. After a couple of entr'actes featuring minor characters, which brought the audience even nearer to the purpose of tonight's occasion, the leading critic started his discourse.

Sue had to admit he did his job well. Long stretches of what he said rose appreciably above the general level – that of an academic lecture in ancient Sumerian – reached by his predecessors. He showed familiarity with Potter's work and what must have seemed to everybody there, except perhaps Potter himself, a genuine love of it. He started his peroration by saying,

'I should like everybody to notice three things about this volume. First, its title. *Off*. Does ˋthis mean that Edward Arthur Potter is off, about to quit the scene and be heard from no more? All of us here, and millions more in the English-speaking world and outside it, hope that this is untrue, and that his unique lyric genius, which has spoken so eloquently for nearly forty years, will continue to delight us for a long time to come. Secondly . . .'

There was a great deal of applause. Sue was good at distinguishing between the polite variety of this, however conscientious it might be, and the enthusiastic. What she heard was unmistakably of the second sort. Potter or his work, however curiously mutated in the process, had reached out beyond the small circle of poetry-readers and the rather larger one of poetry-lovers. She hoped he was pleased.

'Secondly,' went on the leading critic, 'I ask you to look at the dedication. "To all those who have encouraged me to continue in my work as poet." That, I think, is a re- minder many of us need, a reminder of the essential loneli- ness of the creative artist and of his dependence on the under- standing and support of his public. We, representatives of our honoured guest's public, have in the past been shamefully negligent in showing that understanding and proclaiming that support. I hope very much that tonight's words and deeds will go some little way to atone for our neglect.

'Lastly, the content of *Off*, the poems that have been given us. They speak for themselves and need none of my poor help, and all I will dare to do, on behalf of us all, is to salute in them, as in the whole of this great English poet's work, the uniqueness of vision, the distinctive and utterly individual tone of voice that characterize the heart and mind of Edward Arthur Potter. Mr Potter, it is my – '

The ovation, which was what it turned out to be, went on for two and a quarter minutes by Sue's watch. Its earlier moments accompanied the offer and acceptance of certificate and cheque, prolonged for the benefit of the photographers, and similarly prolonged handshakes involving Potter and several of those near him. After that, he stood with his knuckles on the table and his face lowered. Finally, he said in his thick, rather slow rustic cockney,

'My lords, ladies and gentlemen. I'm going to make a short speech, even shorter than the one I'd prepared, because what Sir – Sir Robert has just said fits in so well with what I want to say. As regards those three things he wanted you to notice.

'The title. It isn't really complete. There ought to be another word in front of it. Something – off. A verb in I believe it's called the imperative. It's not my style to come out with the one I'm thinking of in public, but the whole phrase means, Go away. Clear off would be nearly good enough.

'Then the dedication. With respect, Sir Robert wasn't quite right in saying I've been neglected. If only I had been. Right from the start some people have been kind, or what they must have thought was kind, writing nice articles and sending me nice letters. If I had been neglected, I probably wouldn't have wasted my time for thirty-eight years writing what's supposed to be poetry; I'd have looked round for some other way of coping with the state of mind that made me write those things. That's why I'm telling everybody who's ever encouraged me to clear off.'

Potter was speaking now into a silence so total that the sound of individual vehicles in the street outside could be clearly heard. He went tranquilly on,

'Then the third thing, the poems in the book. I wrote them all in a day, just putting down whatever came into my head in any style I thought of, and pretty well everybody thinks they're good, the committee and all sorts of critics and other poets I had proof copies sent to. Or they said they thought they were good. But they aren't good. How can they be? I ought to know, didn't I? Well, that's rather awkward, because if people think they are good, and what's more good in the same way as my previous poems, which fairly beats me, I must say – in that case they don't know what they're talking about and never have known. And in *that* case this, this diploma thing here is worthless, or even a bit of a cheat. You'd think it was a bit of a cheat if, well, if a lot of Eskimos said somebody was a very good cricketer, and we were all supposed to take them seriously. I know I would, anyhow.'

Potter's glance moved in Sue's direction, as if searching for her. She felt frightened and hoped nothing worse was to come. He picked up the certificate and the cheque and held them out in front of him, causing a fresh flurry among the photographers while everybody else sat quiet and still.

'By rights I ought to tear up the diploma, but someone's obviously been to a lot of trouble over it and I shouldn't like to hurt his feelings, so I'll just leave it here. I can't do that with the cheque, because it's a bad thing to leave cheques lying about, so that I will tear up.' He tore it up. 'I don't need the money anyway. That's all. Except I don't want anyone to feel I'm telling him to clear off personally or in any bitter way. It's just a sort of general attitude. Good-bye.'

He was out through the doorway in five or six seconds, yards ahead of the first reporter. Sue was quick off the mark too, but by the time she reached the vestibule she was among thirty or forty vocally bewildered people looking for a vanished Potter. But then, round the corner, she asked the lift attendant for the Essex Room. The man looked at her carefully.

'What name, please, madam?'

'Sue Macnamara.'

'Mrs Macnamara?'

'Yes.'

It was rather like that on the fourth floor, where a door was unlocked from the inside at the news that Mrs Macnamara was outside. Potter surprised Sue afresh by the smartness of his appearance. He said,

'Splendid. What would you like to drink?'

'Could I have a whisky and water?'

'A large tumbler of whisky and water and a bottle of light ale, please.' He relocked the door. 'I thought if you didn't want all the whisky you could always leave some.'

'Aren't you going to have any cornflakes?'

He laughed heartily, showing most of the teeth he had. His manner in general had already struck her as much more confident now than at their previous meeting, almost jaunty. They sat down in a corner on padded straight chairs, face to face across a low table.

'Fancy you remembering that,' he said. 'But then you've got a good memory for all sorts of things. Well, this disappearing act is a bit of fun, isn't it? It's amazing what a few five-pound notes will do. Now we'd better get on. There are some things I want to ask you, and tell you, and we mustn't be too long, because poor Charles, that's my agent, he'll be in rather a state, I've no doubt. It's the first time I've ever done a thing like this, disappear, I mean. Well, and tell people to clear off in public into the bargain. Was that all right, by the way? That was one of the things I wanted to ask you.'

'The clear-off treatment? It was very effective, I thought, judging by the general reaction.'

'Good, but I really meant I hope it wasn't too offensive. You know, wounding. Malicious and all that.'

'I don't think so. You made it clear you hadn't got it in for anyone in particular.'

'Oh, that came over all right, did it? That's a relief. Tell me, my dear, did you find time to look inside that silly old book they were making such a fuss about?'

'Yes, I read some of it.'

'Nothing in it, is there?'

'The last poem made sense of a sort, or the last bit of it.'

'Ah, it's easy enough to make sense of a sort if you don't care what sort. But the book . . . It is rubbish, isn't it?'

'I thought so, yes.'

'I'll take your word for it.' He sighed and smiled. 'That's the most important thing of the lot. Imagine what it would have been like to find you could only write stuff that was any good when you were trying to write rubbish. What a lot of silly donkeys they are, though. Fancy that Sir Robert fellow going on about my individual tone of voice. When I'd purposely made every poem different from the rest of me and different from each other, too. And he's quite clever, you know, that's what frightens me. I've talked to him several times and he's really a very interesting man. But they're all the same. It does seem a pity. Ah, here we are.'

A minute later, locked in once more, they were drinking their drinks.

'What was I saying?' asked Potter.

'About them all being the same.'

'I should have said nearly all of them. There are just a few people, none of them very well known I'm told, who've always said I'm no good. When the publishers and everybody were sending proofs and advance copies round, asking all these critics and so forth for their comments, I made jolly sure those ones, the anti-me ones, all got a copy. Two of them answered, saying politely they were afraid the thing didn't seem to them to merit any special recognition or something. The others didn't answer at all. Another form of politeness. That was a sort of check. If any of them had said it was any good when I knew it wasn't, then they might have been wrong when they said my other stuff was no good. But they didn't. It all fits together. Yes, I think I've proved as conclusively as it can be proved that I've never been any good.'

This was said in the same cheerful tone as before. Sue tried to think instead of merely feel. It took a few seconds.

'But, Mr Potter, that's not the sort of thing that ever can be proved.'

'Not like in geometry, no. Just a very strong presumption. Quite strong enough for me.'

'But . . . you may still be good even though . . .'

'You mean God or somebody may think I'm good. I'd certainly respect his opinion. But he's not letting on, is he?'

'You'll be remembered. Your work will live on. You've been too famous and highly thought of for it not to.'

'When I was a boy there was a very famous man who wrote tragedies in verse. They were very successful – for a while, four of them were running at the same time in the West End. And he was very highly thought of, too. The critics compared him with Sophocles and Shakespeare. He died during the war, the first war that is, just after I left school. He was called Stephen Phillips. Ever heard of him?'

Sue shook her head.

'Neither had Sir Robert when I asked him. And he was born in the year Phillips died. Now isn't that a funny coincidence?'

Both were silent for a time. Then she said,

'Why did you put on this show tonight?'

'That's a good question – I quite see I could have conducted my test and then just privately refused the award. I suppose it was conceited of me. But it was fun. And I felt like getting a bit of my own back on some of the people who'd conned and flattered me into wasting all those years.

And then – this is probably silly, but I might be remembered for a little while just because of this show. Potter? Oh yes, wasn't he that lousy old poet who got together a lot of people who'd said he was good and told them to clear off? A sort of footnote in literary history. Perhaps poor old Phillips might not be completely forgotten if he'd climbed up on the stage at the end of the first night of his *Paolo and Francesca* and told the audience to go and fuck themselves.'

'Yes. Do you want me to report this? Some of it? It could go in our daily.'

'I really don't mind either way. Would you like to report it?'

'I don't think so, Mr Potter.'

'Don't, then. I wasn't telling you with that in mind. I just wanted to tell someone who'd see what I meant. No, more than that. I wanted to tell you.'

'Thank you. How have you been feeling since we met before? You said you were going to – '

'Oh yes. You know, it worked like a charm. The very first lot of pills he tried on me. You can probably see. No more feeling bad. No more wanting to write poems, either. But that's all right, isn't it, in the circumstances? But what the pills didn't take away was this curiosity about whether . . .'

Somebody knocked on the door and rattled its handle. A worried voice called,

'Ted? Ted, are you in there?'

'Hang on, Charles, will you? I'll be out in just a minute.' Potter lowered his voice again. 'He must have used ten-pound notes. Or his intelligence and energy. He's got plenty of all three.'

'They might not have read the book, just going by all your previous – '

'None of them? It's unlikely.'

'Or they might have thought this book was no good and not wanted to hurt your feelings, not wanted to stop you getting the award which they might have thought you'd earned with your previous work.'

'All of them? All saying how it continued the great Potter tradition? Holding a secret mass meeting to agree on a Potter policy? Sir Robert for one would never dream of stooping to anything like that. He's got far too much integrity. What he hasn't got is the ability to tell the difference between a good poem and a bad one. Or even between one kind of bad poem and another. I don't know, perhaps that's harder. Yes. I think in my heart of hearts I must have known I was no good. Otherwise why wouldn't I read my poems when I'd finished them? I'd have read them over and over again very carefully, to try and decide. And of course, I'd decided on the title and dedication of this lot before anybody else had ever seen it.'

'You'll feel differently about this tomorrow. You've given yourself a shock by this test thing of yours.'

They got to their feet as she spoke. Without drawing close to her he rested his hand on her shoulder, having to reach up slightly to do so.

'Do I look shocked? Tonight was just setting the seal on it. I've known the result of the test for weeks now. Don't worry about me, Mrs Macnamara. As I told you, I never feel bad about anything. Not any more.'

3

'Why did he do it, do you reckon?' asked Pat Bowes.

'I don't know. Are we going to make this plane?'

'On our heads. Quit fussing, Macnamara.'

'There's all this stuff of yours . . .'

'So there's all this stuff of mine. Somebody'll have to help me with it. There are men at the airport who earn their livings helping people with stuff.'

Bowes's car, which had a certain amount of Sue's stuff in it as well as a lot of his, hurried westwards down Cromwell Road.

'You're not going to get me off Potter, love. You were one of the last two or three people to talk to him. He must have said something. Or would you rather not talk about it? In which case tell me to shut my jumbo trap.'

'No, I don't mind. I'd have thought it was obvious enough anyway. He felt he'd found out he was no good.'

'That wouldn't make me knock myself off. I know, I'm an insensitive bastard, but there must have been more to it than that.'

'I don't think so. He'd made one gesture, telling his public to go and screw themselves, but that wasn't enough. He wanted to apologize.'

'Apologize? For being just a wee bit offensive to a lot of stuffed shirts who aren't even – '

'No, for being a bad poet, for having spent most of his life doing nothing but write bad poetry, or poetry he thought he'd proved was bad, and wasting everybody's time. He wanted to show he minded. More than about anything else, more than about his wife, which was why he did it in a way that couldn't possibly be mistaken for an accident.'

'Bit rough on the old girl, that part of it.'

'Very. It's the only part of it I don't sympathize with him about, but I can understand. Bad poets mind about poetry just as much as good poets. At least as much.'

'I don't see why it should be at least as much, but you'd know, I suppose. Well, it was a nasty shock. I thought he was a nice old buffer. It's a shame being nice doesn't mean you're good. When I think of some of the talented sons of bitches I've run into . . .'

'I know.'

'You seem to have got on to a lot about him nobody else has. I reckon I read pretty well every word the papers had to say, and there was nothing anywhere near this apologizing stuff of yours, or minding about poetry. You ought to write it up some time.'

Immediately on getting home on the night of the award, Sue had written out everything she remembered – a very large proportion – of her last conversation with Potter. The account was now locked up in her keepsake drawer, with

59

the manuscript of 'Unborn' clipped to it. Certainly she ought to write it up some time; not yet, not until after Mrs Potter was dead. By then, perhaps, it might be possible to see how to write it up, or write it: how best to serve Potter's memory, how to interpret his intention in telling her what he had told her that night. For the present, she felt like somebody ineptly clutching a token of quite obscure significance, a gift with no recipient.

Sue and Bowes continued on their journey in the direction of Peduzzi, who at that moment, it being evening in Ceylon, was sitting in a hut drinking a sort of beer and congratulating himself on the (in fact both pretentious and technically incompetent) piece of film he had shot that day.

R. Prawer Jhabvala

Day of Decision

There was no one else, so Dilip talked to himself. 'I must do it, I must,' he said. He sounded forceful, though he didn't know himself about what. When the old servant brought him his tea, he told him: 'Yes, Chotu Ram, it's time for a change, I've made up my mind. Things can't go on like this.' Chotu Ram took the opportunity to air his own views of life – dwelling mainly on the superiority of the old days over the present deplorable state of affairs – and went on at such length that Dilip, feeling his train of thought disturbed, got irritated and sent him away.

Later he complained to his mother that Chotu Ram was getting too old and garrulous. And the mother laughed ruefully and said 'Old, old – yes, we're all getting old.' So then Dilip was sorry that he had brought up the subject and wished he hadn't; but by then it was too late, for his mother had begun on her own complaints which were mainly to do with being old and not many people caring for you any more and perhaps one was even a nuisance to one's own children. 'Mama!' Dilip disclaimed dutifully, but she said no, it was true and perhaps it was only natural for why should anyone care for the old, they were all too often only a nuisance and younger people had their own lives to lead. Then she said she had this pain again, and Dilip, fighting down his desire to run away, asked 'Which one?'

'The old one.'

'In your knee?'

'No here.' She pressed her hand to her side and looked at him with piteous eyes.

'You want me to call the doctor?'

She made a frail gesture: why put people to trouble? Why bother about an old person? So he went to the telephone and the doctor said he would look in about eleven. His mother was so grateful to him for doing this and became at once so cheerful and affectionate – 'Have you had your breakfast, son? Did they make scrambled eggs for you?' – that he was glad he had indulged her.

But his sister Savira was annoyed when he told her what he had done. 'There's nothing wrong with her,' she said. 'It's only a whim.'

'I know,' Dilip said, 'but –'

'Last week she called him four times. And there was nothing. Absolutely nothing.'

She frowned over her task. She was sorting old sheets, to see which could still be mended and which had to be used up for rags and bandages. She was always busy with some such task. It was she who was responsible for the high gloss and polish on everything in the house, the obedient servants, the punctual, delicious meals. She was a widow, nearing forty, and getting much too fat.

'There's a letter from Vinod.'

She said it in such a way that he knew it contained something special, probably something unpleasant to himself. He waited.

'They are coming next month,' she said, turning over sheets, exaggeratedly casual.

'What, *all* of them?'

'Then what.' She was still very calm. She even spoke with satisfaction, showing him that she, at any rate, was actuated by right feelings and was glad when a visit from their brother and his family was in the offing. But Dilip knew that she was not all that glad either. She had got used to a quiet life and did not care to have her hushed, polished house overrun by a lot of visitors.

And because she knew that he knew her real feelings, she revenged herself a little bit: 'Are you going to the office today?' she asked, looking not at him but only at her sheets and shaking her head over them.

'I may look in,' he answered coolly. He left her and went into the room they called the library because it contained all the books in the house. There were some leather-bound legal tomes dating from the time when their father had studied law, an almost complete Dickens, the *Life of Sri Ramakrishna*, *Princes of India*, and a complete set of Proust which Dilip had once ordered from London and had not yet got round to reading. He put his feet up on the sofa and opened the day's newspapers. He yawned. It was so early in the morning, but he was tired already. No, he would not go to the office today. He did not go most days. No one there wanted or needed him. His brother Virender and a trusted old accountant were in charge. They told Dilip nothing. At one time, many years ago, he had tried to take a closer interest in the family business but all he had succeeded in doing was to get on Virender's nerves. Once Virender had come to the house and had shouted and made a big row; he had shouted at their mother and Savira too, telling them to keep Dilip out of his way and not let him come to the office. Since then, Dilip had hardly gone there; when he did, he shuffled around uneasily in the outer offices and felt like a stranger and was treated as one.

His eyes roved over the newspaper, but he was not taking much in. He said to himself, between yawns, 'I must do it, I must.' He meant he must change his whole life. It could not go on like this. He was not getting anywhere and also he was bored and tired. This was not the way he had imagined things would turn out for him.

Should he get married? When people were married, they seemed automatically to get a lot more respect. Look at Virender, look at Vinod. They were always being held up as examples to him. Yet what had they achieved more than he had? Only that they had households of their own, and wives and children; whereas he was still at home with Mother and Savira and all the old servants and all the old furniture and had not yet struck out on his own. Just because of that everyone thought he was less than they were.

But he didn't really want a household of his own. What for? There were already enough households and enough householders, all leading the same kind of lives and wanting the same kind of things like a new electric ice-cream mixer or a holiday in Kashmir. He had nothing against these things, but he did not think he would want to limit his vision to them alone. And he liked children – he was very fond of his nephews and nieces – and perhaps he would have liked to have some of his own, but finally, well, children were children and then they grew up and then they too would become householders and so it went on. And he wondered: was it enough? Was this what one's life should finally lead to?

So far, he had to admit, his own life led to nothing. Yet there was still possibility: ways were still open to him. It was true, he was over forty, and had lost his figure and a lot of his hair. But inside him nothing had changed. He still loved poetry and music; he was still far too excitable; he was still in love. He folded the newspaper and tossed it aside with the gesture of a man of action. He decided to telephone Amita. Today he would again ask her to marry him. He had often asked her and she usually said yes, but then it never came to anything. Getting a divorce for her meant a lot of trouble, and neither he nor she knew how to set about it; so they just carried on the way they always had done. Usually he was fairly content with that arrangement but not always, and especially not when, as today, he was in a mood of decision.

But on the telephone they told him she was having a bath. He knew that this meant he would not be able to talk to her for hours, because after her bathing she spent a lot of time powdering herself all over with an enormous puff, very slowly and smiling into the mirror as she dabbed. Then she rubbed cream into what looked like wrinkles beginning to form round her eyes, and fondled and oiled the soles of her feet to make them soft, and what was left of the oil she rubbed into her thighs. She did everything in slow motion, lingering over it because she enjoyed it so much. Sometimes she sighed with contentment, and it was all so pleasant and soothing that she became quite drowsy and perhaps even sank down on her bed and shut her eyes, and suddenly she was fast asleep with the little smile of pleasure still on her lips and her oiled thighs spread wide and her hair wet from her bath spread out glistening black on the pillow.

Dilip enjoyed thinking of her like that, but he found it frustrating not to be able to talk to her. He had wanted to so much, not only to settle their future but also to hear her voice purring at him warmly over the receiver and calling him sweetheart, darling, and her own lovely pet. When he thought of her, Dilip felt strong, and hope surged in him that everything could turn out well and life would begin for him in earnest. Only they must be together – without her he was nothing, with her he could become everything. He would be very determined now and force the issue on her. Yes, divorce would be difficult, it would be an obstacle, but what were obstacles for except to be overcome by human strength and resolution?

Savira passed him, carrying a bowl full of roses from the garden. She carried them into the drawing-room and began to arrange them – rather gracelessly, for though she was tidy, she was not really artistic. Dilip had followed her into the room. He was longing to talk to someone and, failing Amita, it would have to be Savira. He said, 'A lot of things will have to be changed.'

Savira didn't say anything, but she appeared to be listening. This encouraged him, for she didn't always have time to listen to him. Often she simply brushed past him, intent on some household task. He went on quickly: 'I must get married.'

'Who to?' Savira said – irritating him, spoiling his

65

mood. As if she didn't know! Everyone in the house, in the family, perhaps in the whole town knew about him and Amita. They had been the way they were for ten years now and had never made a secret of it. For ten years also he had made resolutions to marry her and had often enough told Savira and his mother and everyone else he thought might be interested. And now she said 'Who to.'

He was about to make a sharp retort when she said 'There's the doctor.' Dilip too could hear sounds of arrival, a brisk voice, and then brisk footsteps going to the mother's room. Savira said 'I don't know why you had to call him.' She added: 'Forty rupees every time he comes,' and clicked her tongue in reproach.

Dilip said, with dignity, 'Surely Mama's peace of mind is worth forty rupees,' but Savira had already walked away, following the doctor into their mother's room to see what he did for his forty rupees.

Dilip rearranged the roses in a better way and sniffed them, and then he too went to the mother's room and paced up and down outside the closed door. When the door opened and the doctor came out, followed by Savira, he stepped forward with a correct look of concern. Behind Savira, through the half-open door, he could see the mother sitting up in bed, doing up her last button with a rather smug invalid expression on her face. Dilip walked the doctor out of the house. He paced beside him, his hands behind his back. The doctor was a good deal taller than Dilip, and he also had a finer, more upright figure. He had studied in America and was a respected and fashionable practitioner with many patients who felt proud of and reassured by his American know-how and his calm, confident manner. It was in this calm, confident manner that he now told Dilip, as they walked out of the house side by side in manly fashion, that there was nothing wrong with his mother except nerves and certain inevitable debilities of old age for both of which conditions fortunately modern science had its remedies. The confidence of his tone was enhanced by a certain lightness – a suggestion that nothing need be taken too seriously, everything was under the control of the doctor and modern science, and one could even (so he made clear by an occasional short, rich laugh) afford to be a little bit flippant about these old-fashioned human anxieties. Dilip liked the doctor's tone, and when the doctor laughed, he laughed with him to show how he got the point and was entirely on the same side. It so happened that Dilip did not need reassurance – he knew there was nothing wrong with his mother – but if he had done, he recognized how perfectly the doctor's manner was calculated to give it. He admired him for this. Suddenly he was sure that the doctor was married and had children and lived in a nice house. He admired him for that too. As he watched him drive off in his car, Dilip was fully determined that he too would get married.

But Amita was still having a bath. At least that was what the servant said, though Dilip was sure she had fallen asleep and would now only wake up when she felt hungry. This would not be before quite some time, because before her bath she had no doubt partaken of a very substantial break- fast – she never sat down to a meal that wasn't substantial, it simply would not have been worth her while. He saw that there was no other way but to go to her house and wake her up. He sighed – he would have preferred not to go out but sit around and finish reading the newspaper till Savira would say it was time for lunch. But this was a day of decision, so he had to make some sacrifice. He went to his mother's bedroom to tell her he was going out. He always told her when he was going out, and where he was going, and when he was coming back. Savira also had to be told.

His mother was still lying in bed; she said she didn't feel like getting up. Dilip said 'But the doctor said you were all right.' She shut her eyes. 'Aren't you all right?' She made a weary gesture with her hand. 'Chotu Ram has gone to get the medicine,' Dilip said in the same cheerful voice as the doctor's. But his mother only moved her hand in the way she had done before. How old her hand was, and frail, and the skin loose as if it no longer belonged to the bones. Dilip looked down at his own hand and was relieved to find it plump and firm.

Savira came in with a tray which she put down on the mother's bedside table. 'She hasn't eaten anything,' she said. She stirred around in a cup and held it out to the mother, saying 'Come along now.' The mother turned away her face. 'Do you want me to get angry,' Savira said.

'You must eat,' Dilip said gently.

'I *can't*,' said the mother in a despairing voice.

'Can't, can't,' said Savira, 'what does that mean? You heard what the doctor said: nothing wrong at all. Just nerves, imagination. I could have told you that without forty rupees. Come along now.' And she stirred the spoon relentlessly around in the cup.

The mother's face was turned towards Dilip. To his amazement he saw a tear drop from her eye: just one tear from one eye. Like the skin of her hand, this tear too seemed to be a separate entity, having no connection with the old suffering body that brought it forth.

'Let it be now,' he said. He couldn't bear to look at his mother in case he should witness another tear fall. Instead he looked at Savira; their eyes met, she sighed and put down the cup.

'Vinod is coming,' Dilip told his mother to cheer her up. 'Has she told you?'

'I told her but she wasn't a bit happy,' Savira said. 'I don't know what's the matter with her today.'

'They will make a lot of noise,' the mother complained.

'Is that the way to speak,' Savira said, truly scandalized. The fact that her mother was voicing her own deepest feelings only heightened her sense of outrage. But Dilip was not ill-pleased.

'Well I'm going along to see Amita,' he told his mother. 'Can I get anything for you?'

'What should I want?'

'A nice bar of chocolate?' Dilip said temptingly, but she gave what was almost a cry of pain: 'I can't *eat*.'

Savira said 'This is a new piece of nonsense now.'

'She'll feel better after her pills,' Dilip said. 'Today I'm going to settle things with Amita. We shall definitely get married as soon as she can get her divorce.'

'I don't want any pills,' the mother said.

'They'll be very good for you. You'll see how well you feel. Will you like it when I marry Amita?'

The mother again made that weary gesture with her hand.

'It takes years to get a divorce,' Savira said.

'Not if you have a good lawyer,' Dilip said and got up to go. 'Mama, you're sure you don't want anything? What about a little bottle of eau-de-cologne? To rub on your head for headache? Nice nice,' he said, rubbing his own forehead to demonstrate.

'She still hasn't opened that bottle Virender brought from abroad,' Savira said. 'Will you be home for lunch?'

Dilip hesitated, but only for a moment: 'Yes,' he said. He turned to go without looking at Savira. He knew there would be a tiny expression of triumph on her face: again he had given her proof that the food prepared in her kitchen was better than in Amita's. But there could be no two opinions about that.

It was as he had suspected, and he found Amita asleep in her bedroom. She was even in the same position as he had imagined her – stark naked with her legs apart and her hair spread like a great damp black fan over the pillow. At first she didn't want to wake up, but when finally she opened her eyes, she was happy to see him and smiled and tousled his hair. One thing about Amita, he had never known her not to be happy to see him – the moment she caught sight of him, even when he woke her out of a deep sleep, her face lit up, she smiled so that dimples appeared in her cheeks, and then she made some tender gesture towards him.

69

He sat down on the bed beside her and played with her hair. He unfolded his plan of marriage to her, and she said, as usual, 'All right, darling.' Then a child's voice called her, and she started up on the bed and said 'Quick, cover me.' He looked round and, snatching her silk kimono that lay crumpled on a chair, he threw it over her naked figure, and between them they tugged at it here and there to cover her as decently as possible. Not a moment too soon, for the door had already opened and her little boy came in and asked 'Now what shall I do?'

'Why is he at home?' Dilip asked.

'He has mumps. Did you cut out all those pictures, darling?'

'Come and see.'

'Just let Mummy get dressed.' She winked at Dilip. 'You go with him,' she said and smiled down at herself lying naked under the precariously arranged kimono.

Dilip went with the boy into the sitting-room. Amita's husband was a government servant, and their house was a government quarter allotted to him according to his status. It was to a standardized design but was quite roomy and could have been made attractive if Amita had been less careless and untidy. The room was a mess. Besides the snippets of paper lying around like a snowfall from the boy's activities, there were some other things scattered about that had no place in a sitting-room (such as a tangled ball of string and a broken umbrella). The breakfast things had not yet been cleared away, and there were toast crumbs all over the table and an open pot of yellow jam with a spoon stuck in it.

Dilip admired the pictures the boy had cut out, but at the same time he also looked apprehensively at the boy himself. His jaws were swollen, and Dilip wondered whether mumps was catching. He felt his own glands and asked the boy apprehensively 'Does it hurt?'

'Not now,' the boy said. 'Look at this one.'

'Is it a reindeer?'

'A gnu,' the boy said.

Dilip kept on tapping his glands, first one side, then the other. Was it his imagination, or were they not swollen already? He didn't mind an occasional cold to keep him in bed and coddled by Savira with tasty hot drinks, but he dreaded any real illness, especially one entailing discomfort and pain. As soon as Amita came in, he asked her 'Is mumps catching?'

'Very catching,' she said. 'Haven't you had it?'

'I don't remember.'

Now he was really worried. But Amita didn't seem to think it was anything important. She was admiring the boy's cut-out pictures and advising him what to do with them. Her hair was still loose, and she had a comb in one hand which she occasionally ran through it, attempting to get the knots out. She hadn't worn her sari yet but was in her waist-petticoat and short blouse so that her midriff was bare, and the soft, pale-brown flesh bulged in a fold over the string of the petticoat.

'What about the other children?' Dilip asked.

'They're at school.'

'Have they had it?'

'No, but I'm sure they will all get it now, one by one. I'll buy you a big scrap-book,' she told the boy, 'and on one side you can stick all the mammals and on the other all the – what do you call them – you know, birds and insects.'

'What about fishes?'

'Have you had it?' Dilip asked.

'I've been trying to remember. Probably. I think I had everything.'

'Can you get it twice?'

Amita laughed: 'Why are you so worried? You'll look nice with mumps. Plump and nice.' She made a sound as if she were eating something delicious and tenderly pinched his cheek.

The boy asked, 'Are fishes mammals?'

'I'm not worried for myself,' Dilip said. 'But my brother

71

Vinod is coming to stay from Bombay. What if his children catch it from me? That would be very bad.'

Amita stretched up and ran her comb through what was left of Dilip's hair, murmuring as she did so, 'What a pretty boy.'

'Why can't you be serious!' Dilip cried. 'You're not serious about anything. Not about that other thing either.'

'What other thing?'

Dilip groaned and turned away from her. The boy asked again 'Are fishes mammals?'

'Are fishes mammals?' Amita asked Dilip.

'Some are. For instance, whales. Have you got a picture of a whale?' The boy shook his head. 'I'll get you one. It's a great big fat animal... I've come here to talk to you,' he told Amita in exasperation. 'It's so important but you won't listen.' He thought she was opening her mouth to say something so he shouted, 'Don't ask what about!'

'No, I know what about,' she said. 'Why are you getting angry? Don't you see how much there is on my head? This poor boy sick, and the servant hasn't come back from bazaar yet and there's so much to do.' She dusted a few toast crumbs from the table by way of making a start.

He felt sorry. She didn't usually refer to her domestic troubles, but allowed him to disregard them. When he thought of their relationship, it was only of himself and her he thought, ignoring all the things that went with her – such as her children, this house, the unpunctual servant, the uncleared breakfast table, her husband, and other troubles of whose existence he was not even aware. He felt sorry for her, also ashamed of his own insensitiveness and the way she so readily forgave it. A wave of tenderness for her passed over him and he murmured, 'Let's go in the other room.'

Without another word she turned and walked ahead of him into the bedroom. Her habitual swing of the hips was more than ever evident now that she was not wearing her sari and the great curves could be seen swaying – tic-toc, regularly, with slow enjoyment – within the petticoat. As soon as they got to the bedroom, he embraced her and ran his hands down her sides and hid his face against her neck, tasting the soft skin which she had rubbed with oil and washed with soap and dusted with talcum powder but which still retained its own rich, womanly smell. 'Please marry me,' he said.

'All right, darling,' she said, her eyes shut in pleasure at his embrace.

But he let her go and left her and sat on the bed. 'No,' he said, 'it's not possible for you.' She came and sat next to him with her arms round him, holding him; he looked so sad. She comforted him and he said, 'Why can't we be like other people?'

'We *are* like other people.'

'No – I mean married – always together.'

He thought about his life at home, his loneliness, and his lack of status. He said, 'Till my personal life is settled, I can't get started on anything.' She kissed his cheek with hot lips; her breath enveloped him. But he kept on with his thoughts, and in these he imagined that she was asking him, 'Get started on what?' and he became irritated with her.

'We've talked about it so often. Do you think I'm not serious? There is a lot of scope in the interior decorating business. People are becoming very conscious about interiors.'

'It's a good idea.'

'I intend to read up on it quite a bit. And I told you about the man in the garage who has invented something to do with gears? Of course he's just an ordinary mechanic and needs someone with business know-how to exploit the idea. There's a fortune to be made out of a thing like that.' There were so many possibilities. How often they had talked about it, he and Amita, about all the opportunities that were waiting to be seized! If only he could just settle himself and get his personal life moving on a more dynamic course. It was being with his mother and Savira that kept him back.

'Every day people are getting divorce,' he said. 'It's very common nowadays and not at all difficult.'

Amita was looking at herself in the full-length mirror, exercising her hips by swinging them to and fro. 'I suppose it's too late now to start again with my dancing,' she said wistfully.

'And he'll give. He won't mind.'

'No.'

There was a pause during which Amita undulated her hips.

'How has he been?' Dilip said.

She answered with a light movement of the head to indicate all right.

'He hasn't . . .?'

'No he's been fine.'

Amita's husband was unfortunate. He drank a lot and liked other women, usually of a lower class; he also beat Amita when he was in a bad mood. Sometimes Dilip found her with bruises on her body. How sad he was then! He kissed those bruises and his eyes filled with tears. But Amita didn't make much of it; she even managed to laugh, especially when she saw that he was crying. She tousled his hair and said it was all right. Then she laughed some more and described how she had to comfort her husband in exactly the same way because he too had cried and had felt very sorry for what he had done to her.

'I want to take you away,' Dilip said. He said it with the same anguish and passion with which he had said it for the past ten years. He longed indeed to take her away; also to have her always near him, always for himself. And not only that: 'I have to get married!' he cried. 'Without marriage, what are you? Nothing.'

Amita, still standing before the mirror, now had her hands on her hips. She stamped her feet up and down in the ta-*ta*-ta, ta-*ta*-ta rhythm of the Kathak dance she used to learn. While she was doing this, Dilip suddenly sounded off on the institution of marriage:

'What is it, after all? Merely a hollow social form. And because of this our lives have to be ruined and wasted.'

'It's terrible,' Amita said sympathetically. She attempted some intricate footwork, chanting the rhythm out loud as an accompaniment; from time to time she said in the middle, 'Oh! I've forgotten everything,' disappointed with herself.

'I don't care for convention,' Dilip said. 'I would take you away tomorrow and we would live together and not care one jot for what anyone says. But there are others.' He frowned. 'My sister Savira is a very conventional person. Her first thought is always, "What will people say?" That is her only consideration.' Now that he had started getting angry with Savira, he could not stop, and all her short-comings, all the ways in which he felt she hindered him, came into his mind: 'The only thing she thinks about is how to keep the house clean and tidy. That is what she lives for. How frightened she is that something might be dropped on her carpets, or someone might by some accident scratch the sideboard. If it weren't for her, we could be so comfortable in that house, you and I. There's such a lot of space. I would move out of my room and we would take the big bedroom upstairs.'

'And then the children could have your room.'

'Yes,' Dilip said, attempting to suppress his dismay. He loved to indulge himself in visions of Amita coming to live with him, but he always managed to evade all thought of the children who were attached to her. And indeed it was impossible to think of them living in his house with his mother and Savira, making a noise, stamping up and down the stairs, disarranging the furniture – and that not just for a week or two, as when Vinod brought his family, but for years, for ever – no, it could not be thought of.

'Mother was so strange this morning,' he said. 'You know what she said when she heard Vinod was coming? "They will make a noise." Can you imagine! Her own son and grandchildren!'

'Old people get like that.'

'And Savira pretended to be very shocked. But you know in her heart of hearts she feels the same. I can tell – yes, even though she pretends to be happy and smiles on her face, really she is also thinking of the noise they will make and how they will disturb everything and be a lot of trouble. She is such a hypocrite.'

Amita had given up her dance steps before the mirror. She began to put on her sari. She sighed sadly: 'If only I hadn't been so lazy... I wanted to practise – I liked it – but...' she sighed again.

'You are lazy. Look at the way you go to sleep after your bath.'

'Yes – I sleep, I eat, I listen to the radio – and in the meantime what happens? I get fat – and old –'

'No no.'

'Yes! And you too! Look at you!'

At that, Dilip really looked down at himself. There was no doubt that he too was getting fat. It was all those heavy meals of Savira's; and he never seemed to get time to do any exercise. Perhaps he ought to take up tennis again. He and Amita both: they could go to the club in the evenings and have a game or two.

'Do you still have your tennis racket?' he asked.

'What are you talking about? Here I'm thinking about our life, everything we have become, and you – Go home! I'm tired of you. I don't want you.'

He tugged at her sari to make her sit down with him on the edge of the bed. He kissed a tear from her cheek. 'Why do you think I've come today?' he said in a voice breaking with tenderness. 'Why am I here? Only to tell you that now everything is going to change.'

She did not return his caresses nor did she react in any way to what he said, as if these words had no meaning for her. The boy came in and said 'There is a telephone for Uncle.'

'For me?' Dilip said, looking at Amita in surprise.

'Come here baby,' Amita said to the boy, and as he approached her, she reached out for him, grabbing him, and drew him close to her. She held him tight and kissed his face all over, murmuring 'Mummy's pet, my angel.'

'You shouldn't do that,' Dilip said. 'Not if you're not sure if you've had it or not.'

'Oh go away. Go and take your telephone.'

'It will only be Savira. I suppose she wants me to bring something from the bazaar. As if I'm her servant,' he grumbled.

It was Savira. But a strange, shaking, incoherent Savira: 'Mama's not well,' she said. 'Come quickly.'

At the sound of this familiar voice cracked so strangely under the strain of something unfamiliar, Dilip felt as if his heart dropped plumb through him and with such force that his legs began to shake. His voice became like Savira's, and they spoke to each other like two ghosts: 'Have you called the doctor?'

'He's here. Come quickly. Quickly.'

Amita came out of the bedroom. She looked at his face, and her hand was already poised over her heart ready to clutch it.

'Mother's not well,' he said.

'Is she very bad?'

'I don't know.' But he did know, that was why his legs were trembling.

Amita uttered an appeal to God. Then she straightened Dilip's shirt and smoothed his hair and kissed him goodbye. He remained quite passive and went away; it was only when he was walking down the street that he remembered she should not have kissed him because of the infection.

The first person Dilip met at home was Chotu Ram who was standing by the stairs with tears running down his cheeks. When he saw Dilip, he began to cry out loud and to wail and clutch his head in agony. Dilip went past him straight into the mother's bedroom. The doctor was there, and Virender; they were conferring together, both looking grave and important. Savira was on the other side of the bed, holding the end of her sari in front of her mouth. Dilip went and stood next to her. The doctor and Virender did not seem to have noticed his entrance – at any rate, they went on conferring together without looking up.

The mother looked the same but also terribly different. She had always been small and in old age had shrunk pitifully, but now she looked so entirely wasted that it was impossible to think that this body, as insubstantial as a withered leaf, could ever have sustained any life. And how still she was, what a dreadful lack of movement. Only this morning he had noticed how her flesh had hung from her bones and he had felt sad at this stigma of old age. But that flesh had moved – it had had life in it – and the tear too that had fallen from her eye and had wrung his heart – that too had been warm and had dropped from a human being who had suffered and cried 'No, no, I can't eat!'

'Mama!' Dilip exclaimed and sank to his knees and buried his face in the bed. He cried and sobbed – in great grief and anguish, but also with a strange feeling of relief, almost triumph, that he could do so, that he was alive and had that inside him which could make him feel these terrible human emotions and give expression to them. And through his cries he became aware that Savira too had begun to shout out loud and now she too had sunk onto the floor and was next to him. They turned to one another, and it was good to feel her in his arms and to feel her tears falling on his neck and her bosom squashed against him and heaving with the same pain that was tearing him apart.

Virender was asking for Vinod's telephone number. Savira said she had it written down, she got to her feet and went out with him to put in a long-distance call. The doctor, left alone with Dilip, began to explain to him about the cause of death. He was as calm and confident as ever, just as if he had predicted this all along. The pills he had prescribed for the patient were lying on the bedside-table;

Chotu Ram had fetched them from the chemist, but she had never taken them. Dilip saw the doctor pick them up and look at them with brief professional interest and then put them down again. When he had finished his technical explanation, he ended up, 'Very sad;' but it was not possible for him to look sad because he remained so well-groomed and unruffled and in complete command of any situation that might present itself.

And Virender, now returning from the telephone, gave exactly the same impression, even though his eyes had become a little red. He began to discuss practical matters with the doctor, such as arrangements for the funeral and would blocks of ice be needed to preserve the body till that time. The doctor gave his opinion, and they talked to and fro in calm, manly voices, without taking any notice of Dilip and Savira: not so much ignoring as *sparing* them because they were still weeping copiously and did not look capable of practical thought. Dilip noticed how they left him out, but he did not care. Let them talk, he thought; at that moment he did not esteem or envy them. On the contrary, their preoccupation with practical matters seemed childish to him. At such moments, he thought, it was nobler to be like Savira who was swollen and soggy with tears, gave out short pushing cries like an animal, and beat now her breast and now her head with her fists. The doctor and Virender went on talking about what time the electric crematorium should be booked and the hearse ordered. Dilip's eyes were again on the terribly still figure on the bed. A fly was now buzzing impudently around the face. Dilip waved his hand at the fly without succeeding in chasing it away, and then he too cried out like Savira and began to beat himself about the head.

Chotu Ram came to call him to the telephone. Dilip knew it would be Amita and he didn't want to talk to her. He wanted to stay here with his mother's dead body and grieve over it with Savira. He accompanied Chotu Ram reluctantly. The moment they were outside the door, the servant – quick as lightning in spite of his old bones – went down to the floor to touch Dilip's feet.

'What are you doing!' Dilip cried out.

'Your Honour,' Chotu Ram said, '*Baba Sahib*, I'm your child.'

'Get up.'

'I look only to you. You're now my mother and my father.' And Chotu Ram joined his hands and looked up at his master in humble submission.

Dilip understood that Chotu Ram was afraid there would be changes in the house and that he would be dismissed. At that moment he also understood that he, Dilip, was now master, and that it was up to him to decide whether there would be changes or not, whether the house would be sold or kept on, whether he and Savira would continue to live here or go their separate ways. All this was now up to him.

'Get up,' he said again. He proceeded to the telephone. He picked up the receiver but, before speaking into it, he told Chotu Ram, 'Why do you worry? I'm here to look after you.'

Amita's voice came anxiously over the telephone.

'It is all finished,' Dilip told her with dignity and without tears. 'Mother's gone.'

Amita emitted a cry of shock. Then she began to commiserate with him. Her voice was saturated in love and grief. She told him she knew how terrible it was for him, what it was to lose a mother and such a mother, who had loved him so much; and he had loved her too, he had been a good son and had made her last days happy and that was now his only comfort, if one could speak of comfort in such a loss. Everything she said, and the deep feeling with which she said it, touched him to the depths of his being. He responded to her words with a new gush of tears and with broken words of thanks to her, not only for what she was saying but also for being there to envelop him with her love in this hour of darkness.

Savira came to join him by the telephone. She stood very

close to him. She could hear Amita's voice talking, talking, caressing him over the telephone. Savira did not take her eyes away from his face.

He realized that Savira was looking at him in the same way Chotu Ram had done. She too was afraid there would be changes in the house. And then Dilip himself began to be afraid that things would change – that others would come to live in the house – that their quiet routine would be disturbed – that Savira would no longer be able to cook and care for him. He returned her frightened look, and they gazed wildly at each other, seeking reassurance.

'Darling, my pet,' Amita was saying, 'please speak to me. Say you can bear it.' Savira let out a wail. 'Who's that?' Amita asked.

'She's gone!' cried Savira. 'She's left us!' She clung to Dilip and, calling out to their dead mother, reproached her for going away and leaving them alone like this, two helpless orphans. When she said that, Dilip's grief knew no bounds and, still clutching the telephone, he clung to Savira as she clung to him and they hugged each other's stout bodies and wept together and promised never to leave each other.

'Shall I come?' Amita said. 'Do you want to see me?' And when he didn't answer, she went on, 'It's all right – if you don't want me now, I'll come tomorrow. Whenever you say. Whenever you need me.'

Savira was still weeping copiously, but Dilip noticed that, beneath its grief, her face had taken on the same expression it had worn earlier in the day when he had told her he would be eating lunch at home and not in Amita's house.

Two More under the Indian Sun

Elizabeth had gone to spend the afternoon with Margaret. They were both English, but Margaret was a much older woman and they were also very different in character. But they were both in love with India, and it was this fact that drew them together. They sat on the veranda, and Margaret wrote letters and Elizabeth addressed the envelopes. Margaret always had letters to write; she led a busy life and was involved with several organizations of a charitable or spiritual nature. Her interests were centred in such matters, and Elizabeth was glad to be allowed to help her.

There were usually guests staying in Margaret's house. Sometimes they were complete strangers to her when they first arrived, but they tended to stay weeks, even months, at a time – holy men from the Himalayas, village welfare workers, organizers of conferences on spiritual welfare. She had one constant visitor throughout the winter, an elderly government officer who, on his retirement from service, had taken to a spiritual life and gone to live in the mountains at Almora. He did not, however, very much care for the winter cold up there, so at that season he came down to Delhi to stay with Margaret, who was always pleased to have him. He had a soothing effect on her – indeed, on anyone with whom he came into contact, for he had cast anger and all other bitter passions out of his heart and was consequently always smiling and serene. Everyone affectionately called him Babaji.

He sat now with the two ladies on the veranda, gently rocking himself to and fro in a rocking chair, enjoying the winter sunshine and the flowers in the garden and everything about him. His companions, however, were less serene. Margaret, in fact, was beginning to get angry with Elizabeth. This happened quite frequently, for Margaret tended to be quickly irritated, and especially with a meek and conciliatory person like Elizabeth.

'It's very selfish of you,' Margaret said now.

Elizabeth flinched. Like many very unselfish people, she was always accusing herself of undue selfishness, so that whenever this accusation was made by someone else it touched her closely. But because it was not in her power to do what Margaret wanted, she compressed her lips and kept silent. She was pale with this effort at obstinacy.

'It's your duty to go,' Margaret said. 'I don't have much time for people who shirk their duty.'

'I'm sorry, Margaret,' Elizabeth said, utterly miserable, utterly ashamed. The worst of it, almost, was that she really wanted to go; there was nothing she would have enjoyed more. What she was required to do was take a party of little Tibetan orphans on a holiday treat to Agra and show them the Taj Mahal. Elizabeth loved children, she loved little trips and treats, and she loved the Taj Mahal. But she couldn't go, nor could she say why.

Of course Margaret very easily guessed why, and it irritated her more than ever. To challenge her friend, she said bluntly, 'Your Raju can do without you for those few days. Good heavens, you're not a honeymoon couple, are you? You've been married long enough. Five years.'

'Four,' Elizabeth said in a humble voice.

'Four, then. I can hardly be expected to keep count of each wonderful day. Do you want me to speak to him?'

'Oh, no,'

'I will you know. It's nothing to me. I won't mince my words.' She gave a short, harsh laugh, challenging anyone to stop her from speaking out when occasion demanded.

Indeed, at the thought of anyone doing so her face grew red under her crop of grey hair, and a pulse throbbed in visible anger in her tough, tanned neck.

Elizabeth glanced imploringly towards Babaji. But he was rocking and smiling and looking with tender love at two birds pecking at something on the lawn.

'There are times when I can't help feeling you're afraid of him,' Margaret said. She ignored Elizabeth's little disclaiming cry of horror. 'There's no trust between you, no understanding. And married life is nothing if it's not based on the twin rocks of trust and understanding.'

Babaji liked this phrase so much that he repeated it to himself several times, his lips moving soundlessly and his head nodding with approval.

'In everything I did,' Margaret said, 'Arthur was with me. He had complete faith in me. And in those days – Well.' She chuckled. 'A wife like me wasn't altogether a joke.'

Her late husband had been a high-up British official, and in those British days he and Margaret had been expected to conform to some very strict social rules. But the idea of Margaret conforming to any rules, let alone those! Her friends nowadays often had a good laugh at it with her, and she had many stories to tell of how she had shocked and defied her fellow-countrymen.

'It was people like you,' Babaji said, 'who first extended the hand of friendship to us.'

'It wasn't a question of friendship, Babaji. It was a question of love.'

'Ah!' he exclaimed.

'As soon as I came here – and I was only a chit of a girl, Arthur and I had been married just two months – yes, as soon as I set foot on Indian soil, I knew this was the place I belonged. It's funny isn't it? I don't suppose there's any rational explanation for it. But then, when was India ever the place for rational explanations?'

Babaji said with gentle certainty, 'In your last birth, you were one of us. You were an Indian.'

'Yes, lots of people have told me that. Mind you, in the beginning it was quite a job to make them see it. Naturally, they were suspicious – can you blame them? It wasn't like today. I envy you girls married to Indians. You have a very easy time of it.'

Elizabeth thought of the first time she had been taken to stay with Raju's family. She had met and married Raju in England, where he had gone for a year on a Commonwealth scholarship, and then had returned with him to Delhi, so it was some time before she met his family, who lived about two hundred miles out of Delhi, on the outskirts of a small town called Ankhpur. They all lived together in an ugly brick house, which was divided into two parts – one for the men of the family, the other for the women. Elizabeth, of course, had stayed in the women's quarters. She couldn't speak any Hindi and they spoke very little English, but they had not had much trouble communicating with her. They managed to make it clear at once that they thought her too ugly and too old for Raju (who was, indeed, some five years her junior) but also that they did not hold this against her and were ready to accept her, with all her shortcomings, as the will of God. They got a lot of amusement out of her, and she enjoyed being with them. They dressed and undressed her in new saris, and she smiled good-naturedly while they stood round her clapping their hands in wonder and doubling up with laughter. Various fertility ceremonies had been performed over her, and before she left she had been given her share of the family jewellery.

'Elizabeth,' Margaret said now, 'if you're going to be so slow, I'd rather do them myself.'

'Just these two left,' Elizabeth said, bending more eagerly over the envelopes she was addressing.

'For all your marriage,' Margaret said, 'sometimes I wonder how much you do understand about this country. You live such a closed-in life.'

'I'll just take these inside,' Elizabeth said, picking up the envelopes and letters. She wanted to get away, not because she minded being told about her own wrong way of life but because she was afraid Margaret might start talking about Raju again.

It was cold inside, away from the sun. Margaret's house was old and massive, with thick stone walls, skylights instead of windows, and immensely high ceilings. It was designed to keep out the heat in summer, but it also sealed in the cold in winter and became like some cavernous underground fortress frozen through with the cold of earth and stone. A stale smell of rice, curry, and mango chutney was chilled into the air.

Elizabeth put the letters on Margaret's work-table, which was in the drawing-room. Besides the drawing-room, there was a dining-room, but every other room was a bedroom, each with its dressing-room and bathroom attached. Sometimes Margaret had to put as many as three or four visitors into each bedroom, and on one occasion – this was when she had helped to organize a conference on Meditation as the Modern Curative – the drawing- and dining-rooms, too, had been converted into dormitories, with string cots and bedrolls laid out end to end. Margaret was not only an energetic and active person involved in many causes but she was also the soul of generosity, ever ready to throw open her house to any friend or acquaintance in need of shelter. She had thrown it open to Elizabeth and Raju three years ago, when they had had to vacate their rooms almost overnight because the landlord said he needed the accommodation for his relatives. Margaret had given them a whole suite – a bedroom and dressing-room and bathroom to themselves – and they had had all their meals with her in the big dining-room, where the table was always ready laid with white crockery plates, face down so as not to catch the dust, and a thick white tablecloth that got rather stained towards the end of the week. At first, Raju had been very grateful and had praised their hostess to the skies for her kind and generous character. But as the weeks wore on, and every day, day after day, two or three times a day, they sat with Margaret and whatever other guests she had round the table, eating alternately lentils and rice or string-beans with boiled potatoes and beetroot salad, with Margaret always in her chair at the head of the table talking inexhaustibly about her activities and ideas – about Indian spirituality and the Mutiny and village uplift and the industrial revolution – Raju, who had a lot of ideas of his own and rather liked to talk, began to get restive. 'But Madam, Madam,' he would frequently say, half rising in his chair in his impatience to interrupt her, only to have to sit down again, unsatisfied, and continue with his dinner, because Margaret was too busy with her own ideas to have time to take in his.

Once, he could not restrain himself. Margaret was talking about – Elizabeth had even forgotten what it was. Was it about the first Indian National Congress? At any rate, she said something that stirred Raju to such disagreement that this time he did not restrict himself to the hesitant appeal of 'Madam' but said out loud for everyone to hear, 'Nonsense, she is only talking nonsense.' There was a moment's silence; then Margaret, sensible woman that she was, shut her eyes as a sign that she would not hear and would not see, and, repeating the sentence he had interrupted more firmly than before, continued her discourse on an even keel. It was the other two or three people sitting with them round the table – a Buddhist monk with a large shaved skull, a welfare worker, and a disciple of the Gandhian way of life wearing nothing but the homespun loincloth in which the Mahatma himself had always been so simply clad – it was they who had looked at Raju, and very, very gently one of them had clicked his tongue.

Raju had felt angry and humiliated, and afterwards, when they were alone in their bedroom, he had quarrelled about it with Elizabeth. In his excitement, he raised his voice higher than he would have if he had remembered that they were in someone else's house, and the noise of this must have disturbed Margaret, who suddenly stood in the doorway, looking at them. Unfortunately, it was just at the moment when Raju, in his anger and frustration, was pulling his wife's hair, and they both stood frozen in this attitude and stared back at Margaret. The next instant, of course, they had collected themselves, and Raju let go of Elizabeth's hair, and she pretended as best she could that all that was happening was that he was helping her comb it. But such a feeble subterfuge would not do before Margaret's penetrating eye, which she kept fixed on Raju, in total silence, for two disconcerting minutes; then she said, 'We don't treat English girls that way,' and withdrew, leaving the door open behind her as a warning that they were under observation. Raju shut it with a vicious kick. If they had had anywhere else to go, he would have moved out that instant.

Raju never came to see Margaret now. He was a proud person, who would never forget anything he considered a slight to his honour. Elizabeth always came on her own, as she had done today, to visit her friend. She sighed now as she arranged the letters on Margaret's work-table; she was sad that this difference had arisen between her husband and her only friend, but she knew that there was nothing she could do about it. Raju was very obstinate. She shivered and rubbed the tops of her arms, goose-pimpled with the cold in that high, bleak room, and returned quickly to the veranda, which was flooded and warm with afternoon sun.

Babaji and Margaret were having a discussion on the relative merits of the three ways towards realization. They spoke of the way of knowledge, the way of action, and that of love. Margaret maintained that it was a matter of temperament, and that while she could appreciate the beauty of the other two ways, for herself there was no path nor could there ever be but that of action. It was her nature.

'Of course it is,' Babaji said. 'And God bless you for it.'

'Arthur used to tease me. He'd say, "Margaret was born to right all the wrongs of the world in one go." But I can't help it. It's not in me to sit still when I see things to be done.'

'Babaji,' said Elizabeth, laughing, 'once I saw her – it was during the monsoon, and the river had flooded and the people on the bank were being evacuated. But it wasn't being done quickly enough for Margaret! She waded into the water and came back with someone's tin trunk on her head. All the people shouted, "*Mem-sahib, Mem-sahib!* What are you doing?" but she didn't take a bit of notice. She waded right back in again and came out with two rolls of bedding, one under each arm.'

Elizabeth went pink with laughter, and with pleasure and pride, at recalling this incident. Margaret pretended to be angry and gave her a playful slap, but she could not help smiling, while Babaji clasped his hands in joy and opened his mouth wide in silent, ecstatic laughter.

Margaret shook her head with a last fond smile. 'Yes, but I've got into the most dreadful scrapes with this nature of mine. If I'd been born with an ounce more patience, I'd have been a pleasanter person to deal with and life could have been a lot smoother all round. Don't you think so?'

She looked at Elizabeth, who said, 'I love you just the way you are.'

But a moment later, Elizabeth wished she had not said this. 'Yes,' Margaret took her up, 'that's the trouble with you. You love everybody just the way they are.' Of course she was referring to Raju. Elizabeth twisted her hands in her lap. These hands were large and bony and usually red, although she was otherwise a pale and rather frail person.

The more anyone twisted and squirmed, the less inclined was Margaret to let them off the hook. Not because this afforded her any pleasure but because she felt that facts of character must be faced just as resolutely as any other kinds of fact. 'Don't think you're doing anyone a favour,' she said, 'by being so indulgent towards their faults. Quite on the contrary. And especially in marriage,' she went on unwaveringly. 'It's not mutual pampering that makes a marriage but mutual trust.'

'Trust and understanding,' Babaji said.

Elizabeth knew that there was not much of these in her marriage. She wasn't even sure how much Raju earned in his job at the municipality (he was an engineer in the sanitation department), and there was one drawer in their bedroom whose contents she didn't know, for he always kept it locked and the key with him.

'I'll lend you a wonderful book,' Margaret said. 'It's called *Truth in the Mind*, and it's full of the most astounding insight. It's by this marvellous man who founded an *ashram* in Shropshire. Shafi!' She called suddenly for the servant, but of course he couldn't hear, because the servants' quarters were right at the back, and the old man now spent most of his time there, sitting on a bed and having his legs massaged by a granddaughter.

'I'll call him,' Elizabeth said, and got up eagerly.

She went back into the stone-cold house and out again at the other end. Here were the kitchen and the crowded servants' quarters. Margaret could never bear to dismiss anyone, and even the servants who were no longer in her employ continued to enjoy her hospitality. Each servant had a great number of dependents, so this part of the house was a little colony of its own, with a throng of people outside the rows of peeling hutments, chatting or sleeping or quarrelling or squatting on the ground to cook their meals and wash their children. Margaret enjoyed coming out here – mostly to advise and scold – but Elizabeth felt shy, and she kept her eyes lowered.

'Shafi,' she said, '*Mem-sahib* is calling you.'

The old man mumbled furiously. He did not like to have his rest disturbed and he did not like Elizabeth. In fact, he did not like any of the visitors. He was the oldest servant in the house – so old that he had been Arthur's bearer when Arthur was still a bachelor and serving in the districts, almost forty years ago.

Still grumbling, he followed Elizabeth back to the veranda. 'Tea, Shafi!' Margaret called out cheerfully when she saw them coming.

'Not time for tea yet,' he said.

She laughed. She loved it when her servants answered her back; she felt it showed a sense of ease and equality and family irritability, which was only another side of family devotion. 'What a cross old man you are,' she said. 'And just look at you – how dirty.'

He looked down at himself. He was indeed very dirty. He was unshaved and unwashed, and from beneath the rusty remains of what had once been a uniform coat there peeped out a ragged assortment of grey vests and torn pullovers into which he had bundled himself for the winter.

'It's hard to believe,' Margaret said, 'that this old scarecrow is a terrible, terrible snob. You know why he doesn't like you, Elizabeth? Because you're married to an Indian.'

Elizabeth smiled and blushed. She admitted Margaret's forthrightness.

'He thinks you've let down the side. He's got very firm principles. As a matter of fact, he thinks I've let down the side, too. All his life he's longed to work for a real *mem-sahib* – the sort that entertains other *mem-sahibs* to tea. Never forgave Arthur for bringing home little Margaret.'

The old man's face began working strangely. His mouth and stubbled cheeks twitched, and then sounds started coming that rose and fell – now distinct, now only a mutter and a drone – like waves of the sea. He spoke partly in English and partly in Hindi, and it was some time before it could be made out that he was telling some story of the old days – a party at the Gymkhana Club for which he had been hired as an additional waiter. The sahib who had given the party, a Major Waterford, had paid him not only his wages but also a tip of two rupees. He elaborated on this for some time, dwelling on the virtues of Major Waterford and also of Mrs Waterford, a very fine lady who had made her servants wear white gloves when they served at table.

'Very grand,' said Margaret with an easy laugh. 'You run along now and get our tea.'

'There was a little Missie *sahib*, too. She had two *ayahs*, and every year they were given four saris and one shawl for the winter.'

'Tea, Shafi,' Margaret said more firmly, so that the old man, who knew every inflection in his mistress's voice, saw it was time to be off.

'Arthur and I've spoiled him outrageously,' Margaret said. 'We spoiled all our servants.'

'God will reward you,' said Babaji.

'We could never think of them as servants, really. They were more our friends. I've learned such a lot from Indian servants. They're usually rogues, but underneath all that they have beautiful characters. They're very religious, and they have a lot of philosophy – you'd be surprised. We've had some fascinating conversations. You ought to keep a servant, Elizabeth – I've told you so often.' When she saw Elizabeth was about to answer something, she said, 'And don't say you can't afford it. Your Raju earns enough, I'm sure, and they're very cheap.'

'We don't need one,' Elizabeth said apologetically. There were just the two of them, and they lived in two small rooms. Sometimes Raju also took it into his head that they needed a servant, and once he had even gone to the extent of hiring an undernourished little boy from the hills. On the second day, however, the boy was discovered rifling the pockets of Raju's trousers while their owner was having his bath, so he was dismissed on the spot. To Elizabeth's relief, no attempt at replacing him was ever made.

'If you had one you could get around a bit more,' Margaret said. 'Instead of always having to dance attendance on your husband's mealtimes. I suppose that's why you don't want to take those poor little children to Agra?'

'It's not that I don't want to,' Elizabeth said hopelessly.

'Quite apart from anything else, you ought to be longing to get around and see the country. What do you know, what will you ever know, if you stay in one place all the time?'

'One day, you will come and visit me in Almora,' Babaji said.

'Oh, Babaji, I'd love to!' Elizabeth exclaimed.

'Beautiful,' he said, spreading his hands to describe it all. 'The mountains, trees, clouds . . .' Words failed him, and he could only spread his hands farther and smile into the distance, as if he saw a beautiful vision there.

Elizabeth smiled with him. She saw it, too, although she had never been there: the mighty mountains, the grandeur and the peace, the abode of Shiva, where he sat with the rivers flowing from his hair. She longed to go, and to so many other places she had heard and read about. But the only place away from Delhi where she had ever been was Ankhpur, to stay with Raju's family.

Margaret began to tell about all the places she had been to. She and Arthur had been posted from district to district, in many different parts of the country, but even that hadn't been enough for her. She had to see everything. She had no fears about travelling on her own, and had spent weeks tramping around in the mountains, with a shawl thrown over her shoulders and a stick held firmly in her hand. She had travelled many miles by any mode of transport available – train, bus, cycle-rickshaw, or even bullock cart – in order to see some little-known and almost inaccessible temple or cave or tomb. Once, she had sprained her ankle and lain all alone for a week in a derelict rest house, deserted except for one decrepit old watchman, who had shared his meals with her.

'That's the way to get to know a country,' she declared. Her cheeks were flushed with the pleasure of remembering everything she had done.

Elizabeth agreed with her. Yet although she herself had done none of these things, she did not feel that she was on that account cut off from all knowledge. There was much to be learned from living with Raju's family in Ankhpur, much to be learned from Raju himself. Yes, he was her India! She felt like laughing when this thought came to her. But it was true.

'Your trouble is,' Margaret suddenly said, 'you let Raju

bully you. He's got something of that in his character –
don't contradict. I've *studied* him. If you were to stand up to
him more firmly, you'd both be happier.'

Again Elizabeth wanted to laugh. She thought of the nice
times she and Raju often had together. He had invented a
game of cricket that they could play in their bedroom between the steel *almirah* and the opposite wall. They played it
with a rubber ball and a hairbrush, and three steps made a
run. Raju's favourite trick was to hit the ball under the bed,
and while she lay flat on the floor groping for it he made run
after run, exhorting her with mocking cries of 'Hurry up!
Where is it? Can't you find it?' His eyes glittered with the
pleasure of winning; his shirt was off, and drops of perspira-
tion trickled down his smooth, dark chest.

'You should *want* to do something for those poor children!' Margaret shouted.

'I do want to. You know I do.'

'I don't know anything of the sort. All I see is you leading
an utterly useless, selfish life. I'm disappointed in you,
Elizabeth. When I first met you, I had such high hopes of
you. I thought, Ah, here at last is a serious person. But you're
not serious at all. You're as frivolous as any of those
girls that come here and spend their days playing mah-
jong.'

Elizabeth was ashamed. The worst of it was she really had
once been a serious person. She had been a schoolteacher in
England, and devoted to her work and her children, on
whom she had spent far more time and care than was necessary in the line of duty. And, over and above that, she had
put in several evenings a week visiting old people who had
no one to look after them. But all that had come to an end
once she met Raju.

'It's criminal to be in India and not be committed,' Margaret went on. 'There isn't much any single person can do,
of course, but to do nothing at all – no, I wouldn't be able
to sleep at nights.'

And Elizabeth slept not only well but happily, blissfully!

Sometimes she turned on the light just for the pleasure of looking at Raju lying beside her. He slept like a child, with the pillow bundled under his cheek and his mouth slightly open, as if he were smiling.

'But what are you laughing at!' Margaret shouted.

'I'm not, Margaret.' She hastily composed her face. She hadn't been aware of it, but probably she had been smiling at the image of Raju asleep.

Margaret abruptly pushed back her chair. Her face was red and her hair dishevelled, as if she had been in a fight. Elizabeth half rose in her chair, aghast at whatever it was she had done and eager to undo it.

'Don't follow me,' Margaret said. 'If you do, I know I'm going to behave badly and I'll feel terrible afterwards. You can stay here or you can go home, but *don't follow me.*'

She went inside the house, and the screen door banged after her. Elizabeth sank down again into her chair and looked helplessly at Babaji.

He had remained as serene as ever. Gently he rocked himself in his chair. The winter afternoon was drawing to its close, and the sun, caught between two trees, was beginning to contract into one concentrated area of gold. Though the light was failing, the garden remained bright and gay with all its marigolds, its phlox, its pansies, and its sweet peas. Babaji enjoyed it all. He sat wrapped in his woollen shawl, with his feet warm in thick knitted socks and sandals.

'She is a hot-tempered lady,' he said, smiling and forgiving. 'But good, good.'

'Oh, I know,' Elizabeth said. 'She's an angel. I feel so bad that I should have upset her. Do you think I ought to go after her?'

'A heart of gold,' said Babaji.

'I know it.' Elizabeth bit her lip in vexation at herself.

Shafi came out with the tea tray. Elizabeth removed some books to clear the little table for him, and Babaji said, 'Ah,' in pleasurable anticipation. But Shafi did not put the tray down.

'Where is she?' he said.

'It's all right, Shafi. She's just coming. Put it down, please.'

The old man nodded and smiled in a cunning, superior way. He clutched his tray more tightly and turned back into the house. He had difficulty in walking, not only because he was old and infirm but also because the shoes he wore were too big for him and had no laces.

'Shafi!' Elizabeth called after him. 'Babaji wants his tea!' But he did not even turn round. He walked straight up to Margaret's bedroom and kicked the door and shouted, 'I've brought it!'

Elizabeth hurried after him. She felt nervous about going into Margaret's bedroom after having been so explicitly forbidden to follow her. But Margaret only looked up briefly from where she was sitting on her bed, reading a letter, and said, 'Oh, it's you,' and 'Shut the door.' When he had put down the tea, Shafi went out again and the two of them were left alone.

Margaret's bedroom was quite different from the rest of the house. The other rooms were all bare and cold, with a minimum of furniture standing around on the stone floors; there were a few isolated pictures hung up here and there on the whitewashed walls, but nothing more intimate than portraits of Mahatma Gandhi and Sri Ramakrishna and a photograph of the inmates of Mother Theresa's Home. But Margaret's room was crammed with a lot of comfortable, solid old furniture, dominated by the big double bed in the centre, which was covered with a white bedcover and a mosquito curtain on the top like a canopy. A log fire burned in the grate, and there were photographs everywhere – family photos of Arthur and Margaret, of Margaret as a little girl, and of her parents and her sister and her school and her friends. The stale smell of food pervading the rest of the house stopped short of this room, which was scented very pleasantly by woodsmoke and lavender water. There was an umbrella stand that held several alpenstocks, a tennis racket, and a hockey stick.

'It's from my sister,' Margaret said, indicating the letter she was reading. 'She lives out in the country and they've been snowed under again. She's got a pub.'

'How lovely.'

'Yes, it's a lovely place. She's always wanted me to come and run it with her. But I couldn't live in England any more, I couldn't bear it.'

'Yes, I know what you mean.'

'What do you know? You've only been here a few years. Pour the tea, there's a dear.'

'Babaji was wanting a cup.'

'To hell with Babaji.'

She took off her sandals and lay down on the bed, leaning against some fat pillows that she had propped against the headboard. Elizabeth had noticed before that Margaret was always more relaxed in her own room than anywhere else. Not all her visitors were allowed into this room – in fact, only a chosen few. Strangely enough, Raju had been one of these when he and Elizabeth had stayed in the house. But he had never properly appreciated the privilege; either he sat on the edge of a chair and made signs to Elizabeth to go or he wandered restlessly round the room, looking at all the photographs or taking out the tennis racket and executing imaginary services with it, till Margaret told him to sit down and not make them all nervous, and then he looked sulky and made even more overt signs to Elizabeth.

'I brought my sister out here once,' Margaret said. 'But she couldn't stand it. Couldn't stand anything – the climate, the water, the food. Everything made her ill. There are people like that. Of course, I'm just the opposite. You like it here, too, don't you?'

'Very, very much.'

'Yes, I can see you're happy.'

Margaret looked at her so keenly that Elizabeth tried to

turn away her face slightly. She did not want anyone to see too much of her tremendous happiness. She felt somewhat ashamed of herself for having it – not only because she knew she didn't deserve it but also because she did not consider herself quite the right kind of person to have it. She had been over thirty when she met Raju and had not expected much more out of life than had been given to her.

Margaret lit a cigarette. She never smoked except in her own room. She puffed slowly, luxuriously. Suddenly she said, 'He doesn't like me, does he?'

'Who?'

'"Who,"' she repeated impatiently. 'Your Raju, of course.'

Elizabeth flushed with embarrassment. 'How you talk, Margaret,' she murmured deprecatingly, not knowing what else to say.

'I know he doesn't,' Margaret said. 'I can always tell.'

She sounded so sad that Elizabeth wished she could lie to her and say that no, Raju loved her just as everyone else did. But she could not bring herself to it. She thought of the way he usually spoke of Margaret. He called her by rude names and made coarse jokes about her, at which he laughed like a schoolboy and tried to make Elizabeth laugh with him; and the terrible thing was sometimes she did laugh, not because she wanted to or because what he said amused her but because it was he who urged her to, and she always found it difficult to refuse him anything. Now when she thought of this compliant laughter of hers she was filled with anguish, and she began unconsciously to wring her hands, the way she always did at such secretly appalling moments.

But Margaret was having thoughts of her own, and was smiling to herself. She said, 'You know what was my happiest time of all in India? About ten years ago, when I went to stay in Swami Vishwananda's *ashram*.'

Elizabeth was intensely relieved at the change of subject, though somewhat puzzled by its abruptness.

'We bathed in the river and we walked in the mountains. It was a time of such freedom, such joy. I've never felt like that before or since. I didn't have a care in the world and I felt so – *light*. I can't describe it – as if my feet didn't touch the ground.'

'Yes, yes!' Elizabeth said eagerly, for she thought she recognized the feeling.

'In the evenings, we all sat with Swamiji. We talked about everything under the sun. He laughed and joked with us, and sometimes he sang. I don't know what happened to me when he sang. The tears came pouring down my face, but I was so happy I thought my heart would melt away.'

'Yes,' Elizabeth said again.

'That's him over there.' She nodded towards a small framed photograph on the dressing-table. Elizabeth picked it up. He did not look different from the rest of India's holy men – naked to the waist, with long hair and burning eyes.

'Not that you can tell much from a photo,' Margaret said. She held out her hand for it, and then she looked at it herself, with a very young expression on her face. 'He was such fun to be with, always full of jokes and games. When I was with him, I used to feel – I don't know – like a flower or a bird.' She laughed gaily, and Elizabeth with her.

'Does Raju make you feel like that?'

Elizabeth stopped laughing and looked down into her lap. She tried to make her face very serious so as not to give herself away.

'Indian men have such marvellous eyes,' Margaret said. 'When they look at you, you can't help feeling all young and nice. But of course your Raju thinks I'm just a fat, ugly old *mem-sahib*.'

'Margaret, Margaret!'

Margaret stubbed out her cigarette and, propelling herself with her heavy legs, swung down from the bed. 'And there's poor old Babaji waiting for his tea.'

She poured it for him and went out with the cup. Elizabeth went after her. Babaji was just as they had left him, except that now the sun, melting away between the trees behind him, was even more intensely gold and provided a heavenly background, as if to a saint in a picture, as he sat there at peace in his rocking chair.

Margaret fussed over him. She stirred his tea and she arranged his shawl more securely over his shoulders. Then she said, 'I've got an idea, Babaji.' She hooked her foot round a stool and drew it close to his chair and sank down on it, one hand laid on his knee. 'You and I'll take those children up to Agra. Would you like that? A little trip?' She looked up into his face and was eager and bright. 'We'll have a grand time. We'll hire a bus, and we'll have singing and games all the way. You'll love it.' She squeezed his knee in anticipatory joy, and he smiled at her and his thin old hand came down on the top of her head in a gesture of affection or blessing.

David Zane
Mairowitz

The Police

I was guest of honour at her sterilization. They gave me no
facts. I was told simply to wait in the antechamber, which
was swan's fluff and brass. A pillow's feather had escaped
its pillow and flew about the room, swept by currents of
conditioned air and manufactured wind. I watched it try to
fall to ground, amidst the brass vases and armchairs, all
painted with flowers and pink landscapes. It hung suspended in the breeze and slid the air. I plucked at it to
bring it down. Then I thought better of it.

She had arrived at the penalty. One could never know
the implications. Or the meat of it. There was the penalty to
pay and there was the observation. It was the clarity of the
day. One of the doctors came in and asked if I would need an
injection. I thanked him, thinking not. It was, to be plain,
my second observation. The news caught him up in surprise. He worriedly went to the files. I wondered at it myself,
at the first news, knowing that a second observation always
meant the first was unsatisfactory. I rejected an injection
and watched an old man relinquish himself to his penalty. I
never flinched. In fact I said nothing at all and was con-
gratulated by the doctor in charge. It all seemed a clear and
successful observation. I wondered at my second chance.

The doctor returned with my file. He could find nothing
to support a second visit. Nonetheless, preparations for the
sterilization had been made, and the law required an
observation. There would have to be an ultimate clearance

at some later inquest, but the observation was fixed. He then told me to spread myself face down on the floor pillows and to remain that way until I had physical clearance from the nurse.

It was quite unusual to have to get down on my stomach. There was nothing like it the first time. I sank fast into the thick pillows. There could not have been a mistake. Second observations are always emergency gestures, never required unless the first has been a serious failure. Yet I had done nothing irregular. I thought I had acted admirably, and without an injection. I watched them remove a small piece of the old man's skull, in an attempt to relieve his pressure, a horrible operation in fact, and sat through it all quite calmly. I thought, at the time, the doctors seemed quite amazed at my calm, as if they'd never had a more cooperative observer. Amazing now to find myself on these pillows, awaiting what seemed a criminal clearance.

The nurse entered, announcing that the operation was ready at any time, and only wanted my readiness. I told her I was ready. She thought not. There was interrogation to come. She asked me to relax in my prone position, but under no circumstances to turn in her direction. She was quite pleasant, explaining the importance of keeping the interview completely impersonal. She asked me why I passed up the invitation to injection. I told her of my composure on the first occasion. She asked me why I had been called a second time. I explained my own confusion about it. Had I any strong physical reaction to the old man's penalty? None whatever. She admitted, unofficially, that she couldn't understand why I'd been summoned. Then she asked me if I enjoyed the swan's down pillows. I said I wasn't quite sure I enjoyed my position on them. Then I noticed the feather still floating in the air and called it to her attention. She assured me it was not a matter for concern. Did I understand the process I was about to witness? I didn't know. Did I ever want children of my own? I'd never given it much thought. Did I enjoy the swan's down pillows? I said I'd answered that question. She told me to answer again. I said they were comfortable. Then she wondered whether the operation would lead me to stimulation. I couldn't see why it should. She said it was not worth the risk on my part, and besides she had been given instructions.

She told me to lower my trousers and again I insisted I was quite all right without an injection. She told me to put my hands above my head. She pulled my trousers to my ankles. I was quite embarrassed, but even more disturbed that she had become severe. She placed what felt like a thin rough institutional towel beneath my genitals and, to my surprise, began to manipulate me. I turned my head to her and she shouted in sharp reproach. I turned away again. Still she manipulated me and I could feel my face flush of it. I said I was sure it wasn't necessary and by this time she stopped answering. Quite methodically she pulled at me, her arm thrust under me, from behind and between my legs. Her hands were rough with the touch of perhaps old and dying patients, restless mummies in their whinings and bed-pans. My body began to move with the rhythm she made, so she held me fast to stop me, with her free hand at the nape of my neck. I felt like a female cat. Finally, she spilled me onto the towel and, instinctively, my hand came down from its assigned position to meet hers. But she drew away, ordering me to clean myself quickly and get dressed for the observation. I turned and she was gone. As I stood up my imprint faded off the swan's down pillows which seemed to float back to attention. In my hand I held the evidence of my spillings.

Once washed and dressed I sat down again in the antechamber. I felt cold and flushed. Thought quickly to pull together and make a good impression. I knew a third observation was the penalty itself.

The first doctor came in and led me to the operation chamber where I was greeted cordially by the other doctor, who was in charge, and the nurse. The head doctor asked

me again if I wanted an injection. I said I felt well enough
without it. He asked me why this was my second observation. I said I thought he would know better than I. In
fact, he said, he did not. He had read the files but there was
no evidence of trouble there. Surely I had some idea about
it? None, I answered. There would have to be an inquest,
he said, but for now it was essential to get on with the
operation. I told him I agreed.

I still felt quite weak as they sat me in the guest of honour's
chair. The ordeal with the nurse had quite humiliated me
and I worried that I might still be trembling and that it
would be noticed.

The prisoner was wheeled out on a brass operating
table, which was placed about two yards from me. I was
surprised to find her conscious. She stared about in seeming
unconcern, scarcely moving, unalert, clearly drugged. I
imagined her face was wild and unruly in her natural state.
She was guilty of some public acts of distortion; this was as
much as I, the observer, could be told. For me, it was
enough. On the brass table her hair was the colour of olives.

One final time I was offered an injection. Again, I de-
clined, though I was still not completely myself. The doctor
warned it was not a pleasant operation. I worried for a
moment whether I was giving too much resistance, but, in
the end, I insisted I would be all right.

The doctor then told me to join him at the operating
table, where he threw back the sheets and revealed the girl,
naked. I watched calmly as he spread her legs to my view,
knowing quite well I was being watched myself. There was a
plastic tube protruding from the girl which, the doctor
explained, went from her vagina into the region of her
ovaries. Was I concerned at her pain? I said I could not be
concerned if it was part of the penalty. The nurse asked if
the girl's body aroused me. I said it did not. So many ques-
tions, unlike the first time when I was left alone to my
observing. I presumed they would all have to answer ques-
tions about me at the inquest and were preparing their

analysis. I tried to assure the doctor-in-charge that there was no need for concern, and that I was really quite capable of containing myself at these or any other proceedings. He smiled and said he thought so too.

I was then told to resume my seat and wait until the two doctors and the nurse had conferred. Before they went into the antechamber, the nurse turned the operating table in such a way that I was faced with the tube and the girl's legs. I saw it was not enough that I'd already proven myself. This was yet another test. After a time, the girl twisted and fell onto the marble floor. She had not been strapped in, I thought, in a moment of panic. I leaned forward, but then thought better of getting up. I sat back and waited. I was still cold from the air-conditioning and imagined how much colder the naked girl was. She lay on the floor, helpless, gaudy tubes displayed, and in pain. Outside, they were wasting the precious moments of her anaesthesia in testing me. The girl opened her drugged eyes at me and said nothing with them, although I expected some condemnation. Then I thought I recognized something olive about her, knowing her somehow and somewhere.

The nurse and doctors came in and broke my recognition. They lifted the girl back onto the table. The head doctor smiled and seemed pleased with the way I handled the situation. I was relieved.

The nurse announced the girl would get no more anaesthetics, and what did I think of that? I asked her to repeat the question. She had taken me by surprise in my relief. She repeated the question. I said it made no difference to me if they thought it best. I wondered if that was too vague a response. I was still being tested. The head doctor asked me if I understood how the operation worked and I answered no. He showed me an object that looked like a small fat pistol. It was a radium gun which, when fired through the tube inside the girl, would annihilate the immediate tissue and burn out her ovaries in a slow radioactive heat. Did that disgust me? Not in the least, I assured him. He claimed it was so simple anyone could do it. Would I care to try? I stumbled over my response momentarily. I did not feel competent. It was really quite simple, he insisted. Then I braced in my chair and said I would do it if he ordered me to. He said he would not do so. It was up to me to volunteer. I thought it was quite irregular since an observation was supposed to be just that, and participation in the penalty out of the question. To which he replied he had no intention of letting me fire the pistol, but merely wanted to know if I would like to. In confusion, I said it would be interesting to try. He turned to the others and smiled. I believe he was trying to help me against the suspicions of the others. He walked back to the table, seemingly content, placed the pistol in the tube and pulled the trigger. The girl moved gently at first, then screamed so loud that I moved sharply in my chair. I looked up quickly. No one had noticed. I tried to compose myself, but the scream had unnerved me. I imagined the heat inside her, burning away her sex. It would calm her distortions, I hoped.

The girl moaned in pain and twisted her head again toward me. I thought perhaps I knew her, although it was unlikely. Great precautions were always taken to insure that the observer had never seen the prisoner before and had no knowledge of the prisoner's act. But I thought I recognized her face and olive hair, an image of her under an olive tree, somewhere perhaps in a photograph. Still I would have been sure of it, there not being many like her. I was, nonetheless, increasingly aware of her presence as she moaned. Could it be?

A second shot was fired and she screamed again, this time leaving a whistling sound in my ear. I sat calmly, I'm sure of that, even though confused in my thoughts. I lowered my head and stared at the marble floor for a moment. Who was she and why this haunting? The whistling continued.

The nurse stood over me. She had caught me with my head down, but I responded promptly when she said I was wanted at the table. There the head doctor told me he had to fire a final shot, but he could tolerate no more screaming. Therefore, he asked me if I would kiss the girl to hold her mouth and tongue. The girl looked at me and stared in what was unquestionably a moment of recognition. She knew me and was telling me so with her eyes. She was asking to be kissed. The doctor said I should kiss her and, to be perfectly lawful about it, I asked him if it was in order. He asked me if I wanted to do it and I said I would not do it if it might be irregular. He laughed quietly, convinced, I'm sure, of my clearance. He then ordered me to kiss the girl's mouth shut.

I wanted to take the time to look at her closely, but I didn't dare jeopardize my chances. I fell onto her mouth and held her lips with mine. It was not a real kiss but it had been so long between the touches of a woman's mouth that it might just as well have been ecstasy. I could feel the nurse's eyes on me. But my face remained pinned to the girl's, without moving, expressing nothing. Then the third shot must have been fired, for I could feel the contractions in her face. She made a whining noise, which is all I allowed her, and suddenly, somehow, seemed to thrust her tongue into my mouth. She held me with her tongue, drawing mine further into her mouth until I choked and tried to pull away. Then she bit my tongue and held me hard. I could see drops of blood spurt onto her face. Then she relaxed momentarily, kissed me gently, and let go of me.

Coming up for air, I knew I must make a good show. My tongue ached and the blood trickled from my mouth. I tried as well as I could to show I had come through even this ordeal. The nurse handed me an institutional towel and I bled onto it.

They told me to sit down in the place of honour again and I did so, still clutching the towel. I stared at the girl. Her face still troubled me, though it was now the memory of her mouth that filled me. In the back of my mind there was some recognition of her, but it was dim and fading with her taste in my mouth. They were sweet memories, no doubt, but lost among the varied clarifications of living now. The nurse asked me if I was finished with the towel. I gave it to her. She smiled in such a way as to tell me I was lost.

The doctor-in-charge came to me and read the usual formalities about how fortunate I was to be given the opportunity of observing. The penalty was serious and unfortunate, but it was the penalty.

I watched the second doctor remove the tube from the girl. It seemed endless and I felt depressed at it. It was a gloom I had inherited, it was bleak thinking, unnatural to me. And uncomfortable.

After the formalities, to which I hardly listened, knowing all the words myself, the head doctor walked with me to the street, speaking all the while of the operation. Outside he told me, informally, it was the best observation he'd ever seen. He was quite amazed at my composure and good sense throughout. He wasn't sure he could have acted as well himself. There was no question that the inquest would go off splendidly. Inside our smiles, both of us knew he was lying.

David Zane
Mairowitz

The Grace

Born a boy, she would have been Franklin Delano Roosevelt Munch. Instead she was named to commemorate her own illegal entry through popular evidence of gloomy weather, a song of mournful lovers, she, Perfidia, the woman-child, disgrace and burden to a history of doctors and certified public accountants. Her opening leap into being had rent a significant hole in Mother Munch, awaiting a masculine sonata at the first scream. She had been cheated of her seasons and her purpose. And when, with the first dive for the breast, the child drank down her feast and kept it down, without a moment's falter at the brink of catastrophe, with a giggle of containment and unconcern, the perfidy was complete. Mother Munch was left in the lurch.

Perfidia always held fast to her vision of the 1940s, a time when she was talked out of her childhood and subtly prepared for that dark night of the womb in which she must linger till the menopause. It was a time of commitment and War, clearing the table momentarily of a previously dispassionate existence. And somewhere after the War (her Mother warned) she would bleed from the loins, to do penance for being born a girl. The War had taken all the boys away (including Father Munch, who returned quickly with shards of exploded metal in his thigh) and the women were barren and empty for a time. 'The horror of a world without men,' cried Mother Munch, in such a manner as to leave no question but that Perfidia was guilty of it.

And, after the War, Father Munch would have no sons

what with his mangled thigh, and the woman-child was stretched to the borders of her life. There at the edge she was to accept responsibility for this final outrage against history and drift into a melancholia which would pursue her through all the journeys back to her centre. At age nine she lost her innocence to a migraine headache which served her up spent to her impending womanhood. This pain hung on her eyes like fishweights, pressing their soft jelly in an illicit caress.

And yet, it was not to be spoken of. Too much suffering had already spread from the contagion of her existence. There was Father Munch, taking her for long walks in the woods, limping his post-war limp, hardly speaking aloud, muttering to himself and wiping the occasional tear. The mine-blast had lifted him skyward, and now he thought he floated over the 1940s in a slow leak, soon to spread-eagle thud on the infected marshes of his life.

Still, something remained with her of these desperate afternoons, some vague hint of sentiment in the aftermath of the War. It was as if coherence was a fact, not a luxury, the men were home, babies were appearing on the landscape and the mediocrity of the coming decade had not yet cast its tentacles.

Perfidia dreamed of the day she would have long legs and wear broad-shouldered gowns.

A memory of razors clings in the wedges where her eyebrows have been removed. 'Prince Kropotkin' had shaved them himself, despising, as he did, the hair on women's bodies. She needed grooming, an overhaul. She had let herself run down. He would change all that. With his razor he would carve out the New Woman. His legs had wrapped round her head, holding her fast, while he lathered her brows, softened them with his fingers and finally danced over them with several turns of his wrist. She bled, but never screamed. She had summoned this pain and devoured it at the roots.

After which he commanded she lose weight and she starved for weeks to no avail.

His name was Zimmerman, but these were clandestine desperate days. He had pinned her beneath him like a butterfly, his meat hands wrapped round her wrists, ankles chaining legs. And boxed under glass she could look up through the surface at his man's face, thick and bearded, and wonder, in the paste of her dilemma, how she had managed to will it. In the night he would come and go, this, her first lover, pressing at her corners with his massive demands, leaving her stretched and disfigured to the secret mirrors inside her.

Five years on, his steel has welded to the iron terror of her migraine, a permanent fixture in her eyebrows. The hair has never grown back and she is marked as a fifteenth-century concubine. The old concentrate of blood leaves her puffed and swollen and, in her newer mirrors, she sees the corpse of her worn pride and bends in the accepting.

'Now we start with a steel pipe, maybe four inches in diameter and eight inches long and we cap it at one end. We fill it three quarters full with ammonium nitrate, then equal layers of potassium chlorate and confectionery sugar on top of that.'

His hand runs under her blouse and massages her nipples as he talks. She takes in five years of him in one breath, his hand has changed, roughed over with gunpowder. She feels the sting of his assassinations in his triggerfinger. He is roving in the zone now and encounters the switchblade knife strapped to her belly. He intuits five years in that touch. He is amused. In her depths she contemplates drawing the blade across his eyes. Yet she hasn't the simple words to stop his fingers which have now found her out. She is stretched, they note, widened beyond contempt.

'You aren't listening.'
'I am.'
'You were daydreaming.'
'No.'

'It's always the same, isn't it? You want to perform, to open the floodgates, move out of your quicksand. But when it comes to the crunch, you haven't got one minute's concentration.'

'I'm ready.'

'If it were up to me, this wouldn't be assigned to you.'

'Why?'

'You haven't got the fluidity. Emergency washes over you like a sandstorm... You cap the open end with a primer made with a high-powered rifle-bullet, .30-06 preferably, with as small a lead slug as possible. Now we cut off the slug right here where it joins the shell casing. Then drill a hole in the pipe cap the exact size of the bullet, then seat the bullet in the hole, leaving about one third of the bullet primer sticking out. Now we come to the fuse... You can't fake this one, babe. Why they've assigned you such an important event I don't know. Maybe they think you can handle it 'cause you don't know the fear of the game yet. But it's foolproof if you can muster the attention, the pride. Everything will be prepared for you. It can only fail if you do. Understand?'

'No.'

'Figure it out. You think you can handle this?'

'I said I was ready.'

'Ready for what? Ready to understand, ready to go in, willing to do this for us? The others seem to have confidence in you. I don't think you'll ever make it.'

'Why not?'

'Because you're blocked. Between one end of this manoeuvre and the other is an incredible momentum.'

'And so?'

'Your rhythm's all wrong.'

The ghosts are howling in the wind of her headache. He gunned, slammed the cycle into gear and they were off along the furious cliffs. Against the grain of the wind her wispy masses of hair danced out over the canyon, wrenched from her temples and pulled violently along her scalp. Down below she saw a multiplicity of possible deaths, brains shattered about the perimeter in hairpin spins of the bike. Her own corpse strewn about the valley in a thousand breakings. They were the pieces of her and each was like soft fur caressing the whole of her as she stampeded the dustbowl. Every joint ached in her coming-alive and she was inspired to bend her weight toward the brink in order to feel the deathglide through unfriendly space, a collapsing in air, the acceptance of her fall, the split-second preening for the act of impact. And the prepared strength in the certainty she would never scream.

He was content to murder frogs with his pistol. The brook lay stretched below a dark cliff and he casually fired at frantic amphibians. When he was bored, he fired first to the side of the frog, hoping to nail it in mid-leap with a second shot. Then he told her to take off her clothes which she did without protest. Did she have protection? She didn't understand. He had a rubber, he said, but didn't feel like using it. What did she think of that? She didn't think anything. Keep your pants on. It was more fun that way anyway. The sun was melting her brain and, like paste, she glided wherever his fingers spread her. And soon he was battering at her through her underwear and she lay thoroughly clutched and unmoving. She could feel the soft cloth tickling her inside and quickly his moisture gathering in her. More than that she could not answer for. Where's the blood, he demanded. She had nothing to give him, not even this desperate gesture to nature. He cleaned himself in her hair and she was forced to wash it in the brook so that on the return up the canyon it no longer sailed behind her like a mare's-tail, but cracked wet and heavy on her back like whips.

'You need some mending-tape about three eighths of an inch wide. Now you dissolve equal amounts of potassium chlorate and sugar in boiling water. The solution must be strong but not saturated. Soak the tape in the solution and wrap it round the cartridge base, making sure to get as many turns of the fuse as you can. When it dries your fuse will burn at about two minutes per foot.'

His hand is now on her head and his fingers are laughing over the new-shorn fuzz of it. Crudely shaved at the neck, she will need a wig for her performance.

'You will need some straight clothes.'

'I haven't any money.'

'That's your problem. You'll need hair and make-up too. See to it. . . Finally, you must shape the charge to direct most of the explosive force in one direction. Grind away the centre of the first pipe cap and place this end against your target. Now, what are you going to do with it?'

'Blow the . . .'

'Wrong already. This bomb I've described to you is crude. You will have to learn to construct one in an emergency, in case something goes wrong with the more sophisticated explosive you are given. You need to gear for an emergency, Perfidia. Everything depends on it.'

He inspects her teeth, forcing his nails into her gums till they bleed. Five years of murdering statesmen and executives, police officers and informers probe in her mouth. She gags. He checks her ears, still caked with wax, finds those areas of her body he knows will be coated with filth. She will have to preen, but now, for a moment, she challenges his thrust. He can fuck himself. Nonetheless, she is told, she will preen for the Movement, for her task she will wash, diet, bend and buckle. Finally, she will leave her door ajar this night.

In the night she is visited by her migraine, and it enters her via the ports of her eyeballs. This is her 'troll-lover' who has latched himself onto her face, probing the secret reaches of her nostrils, her mouth, her eyes and ears. He has kept the fine hours of her life and caused her unceasing grief. Look now as he carries her to the multiple Academies of her youth, houses of desperate worship where purpose and achievement are sanctified. It is to these concentration camps that Mother Munch forces her, the proving-grounds of her fantasies of the future. Yet Perfidia is strangely at home here what with the festering values of a century fixed and on permanent display, a museum-mirror to her casual self-eradication. Here she learns the root and seed mythologies, the preponderances of the family, the dominion of the State. Here she is made to understand that life is an accumulation of its pressures ('the competition's fierce, babe') and that Man is in a perpetual state of war with Nature, thereby rendering a life of achievement a full-scale battle. We must earn our place, she discovers. We must grow in the process, we must gather the distressing threads of social history and carry them into a future of concrete accomplishment. Still, she feels more like a witness giving evidence to her days.

She also learns that woman is now emancipated and that she must take her place alongside man in the creation of diplomatic channels to the Natural State. She must employ the tools of femininity to summon up pathways to power which end of necessity at a better world. All this she must do in the understanding that the elements of her search and vision will certainly be hostile to her, that she must establish her values and hold them to her bosom, that force and determination are gestures of survival in the landscape of stress.

Yet she is pinned to the wall by migraine. The years wash over her in waves of pain and she walks the tombs of the Academies in simulated catatonia. Her troll-lover is antisocial, this she knows. She stands in gloomy courtyards in moments when he has taken hold of her eyes and casually dreams the stones to dust. He has loaned her the will to destroy all this and she carries her secret to the peripheries of knowledge – and escapes. Mother Munch will not hear of it and conjures up her riot squads. They trace Perfidia to the borders but she has disappeared inside herself, dropped to the depths of her well with her troll-lover who presses her eyeballs to a blindness in the darkness. Mother Munch goes into mourning for her own life, for the perpetuation of her image.

Prince Kropotkin has pushed open her door. She has lain between sleep and torment all night. She did not expect him, yet she has left the door ajar. She did not want him, yet she has left the door ajar. The pain leaps about her face like light.

Her eyes begin to focus in the light now violently switched on. She sees a second man, vague. He has escaped the armies to the East and joined the Movement. He has contacts in military munitions warehouses. A history of such Comrades tells her she must be his whore. She rushes toward sleep. The sheet is pulled back, and she is exposed sweating and unkempt. Kropotkin indicates where he has shaved her brows, then proceeds to massage her body. He bridges five years. She sweats, cannot summon, yet again, the language to distract him. He offers her with a simple gesture of moving away. In her half-sleep she blocks comprehension of it.

Kropotkin stands at the window, looking for his police-shadow, speaking of the Movement. Like the soldier, he has learned to harness his aggression and employ it to purpose. He has lived the thrill of random violence and run it aground. He has now read the texts and understood. The Comrade has mounted Perfidia and is in her instantly, before she wakes. She is his first woman since the War and he is spent before her body can even yield to its pleasure. Now she is awake and crying in this, and she is made aware of a black body spinning from her. In his controlled fury, Kropotkin reminds her she has never understood. Then too, she is weak and demoralized. He will take his turn, but only in disgust. She jumps from the bed and flicks open her knife. The soldier immediately disarms her, then demonstrates how to avoid being disarmed. Kropotkin claims she has learned nothing about self-defence and must join his lectures in karate and weaponry at the Women's Brigade. Again he tells her she will fail in her mission. She hasn't the scope, the range, the sense of humour. They leave her to her migraine. She weeps. She closes, locks the door in anger and contempt. Somewhere in the night, a night of narcosis, she awakes, a sleepwalker to her mythology of regret, and leaves the door ajar once again.

'Your pistol is your lover, ladies. Wear him close to you at all times like a protector. If you forget that for one minute, you may find yourself shot down defenceless.'

The women resent his patronizing, but his expertise is essential. He has run these guns himself, armed and taught the entire Brigade. Then too, he has instructed them in the practice of yoga and isometric exercises, military callisthenics and jiu-jitsu. Kropotkin's proficiency and commitment are legendary in the Movement. His practical fame has spread like a contagion among the women who have known his prying palms. Each has had the hatred of him and yet he holds an apocalyptic future over them all with his military gifts. Each has dreamed a secret ice-pick in his brain, but still spreads before him now in callisthenic humiliation, underarms pouring sweat to his signals.

Like a sack he dumped her on the porch of Mother Munch's and kicked her belly again and again, craving one instant of protest, one murmur of repudiation to wash him clean. But she continued to deny it and the torture bent and crippled him. He knew it wasn't pride for she had none, surely. He banged her head on the wooden porch till she lost consciousness and he threw her in a hedge.

When Mother Muncn discovered her there, she would not talk. She was tranquillized, put to bed and, in the night, he broke in where she slept and climbed on her, smacking against her insides like a steam-hammer. Afterwards, he injected some morphine and cried on her hair, wiping his eyes and nose in it. He told her of his electro-therapy, designed to squash his fury, but it had come to nothing. All his life he fought for the mastery of his body. His control had failed, his will had gone rotten, he was afraid of killing her. She didn't care. Why didn't she fight him? Did she love him? She didn't know. He would teach her to stand up to him. He would teach her pride. What did she think? Nothing.

In the light, Mother Munch discovered him in Perfidia's bed and threatened him with Authority. It was the last the two women had seen of one another and the elder, some years a widow, found her solace in the charting of astrological bodies in their pilgrimage across the arcs and chains of the heavens. This way she could no longer proclaim, only guess. In this new gift, she uncovered the safety of the Moment, a clear picture rising before her in the day, and waived her rights at last to the frantic future.

Perfidia cracks under the strain of this morning-after and her body's stress. Kropotkin makes an example of her before the others, demonstrating how she has been assigned the most momentous task of all and hasn't one-half its necessary resources. She sits in a frothing heap as he stands over her, lecturing the Brigade on their habits. They are all fat and beneath the contempt of the Movement. From this day, they are to consume twice the normal protein or give up the struggle. Carbohydrates are to be cut to a minimum and the working day is to be divided into clear thirds, bodily upkeep, weapons practice and careful reading of the classic texts. Intercourse, also, must be kept to a minimum, as it will drain the vital energy banks. At the same time, sexual frustration is to be avoided as it makes for muscular imbalance. Narcotics are out of the question, as well as alcohol. He will only lend his service and his proficiency to a disciplined Movement. He then suggests a meeting to strip Perfidia of her role and replace her with a more capable Comrade. She turns on him like a scorpion. His teeth are waiting for her rebuttal. They glisten damply and persecute her in their bite. Another sister protests on her behalf. The choice has been made. He is to take no part in the selective process, but restrict himself to training. There is to be no vying for power or intercommunal combat. To replace her would mean a severing of respect and commitment. The sisters assent. He bares his teeth once more. Perfidia attempts to whitewash any intentions written on her face. She stands to him, but her belly contracts in the signal that her period has begun. He can see this and bends to her agony, examining her fingernails.

'It is lucky for you. Five days from now you must perform and will have stopped bleeding. In that time you will also stop using tobacco or picking the skin from behind your nails. You will also go into solitary confinement in three days time, take all your instruction and exercise alone and you will be known now, for better or worse, as Rosa Luxemburg.'

The broad shoulders of the forties contracted, then flamed into the conical breasts of the fifties. Perfidia never got her gown and silently went into mourning for it. Her decade had run down and given way to whitewashed times. A mediocre moan hung on the wind, a tuneless echo, low and dishonest. One day during these terrible times she began to bleed from the loins and, at last, the prophecy had come true. She had brought this upon herself and nothing would change it. She crept through the halls of the 1950s, a hungry voiceless spirit. Toothless men embraced her in the streets and she carried their whiskey-breaths to her terror-caves. They fumbled in her underwear in dark parks and their fingers clung to her regions long after, in her solitude. And, in an era of perpetual accusation, Perfidia said nothing.

Father Munch spent these days before the smiling image of a bald man who had led him to battle, and adopted the fear of the moment. He felt accused. The fingers on the screen pointed at him, a broken soldier, as the war penetrated the bowels of the Eastern jungles. Then, as quickly, he willed a cancer in his brain and waited for the times to take him. His demise was silently laid at Perfidia's doorstep and, for retribution, she conceived a skinful of ugly protrusions. This was intolerable to Mother Munch who, having long since given up the notion of a future for herself, began to groom the daughter for an inevitable merger. Four days a week under the sun-lamp, a dozen creams and ointments, but Perfidia's stubborn persona failed to yield up its facial fruits. Then brushed and combed, vaginally deodorized, caked with paint, small breasts uplifted in tight brassieres, revealing pastel sweaters, nightly pin-curls, the package was as complete as it might ever be. Still, the demons of Perfidia resisted and an ungainly, plump and marked specimen emerged from Mother Munch's machine. It was further evidence to the crimes of existence she had perpetrated from the starting-gun.

A sort of reverie takes the old woman as she watches over the chainlock entrance. It is a face she knows, evidence of an old pox, features unwashed, unkept. From out of some dim conjunction of planets a face has presented itself in the four inches of chainlock evidence-space and breeds in her a sudden paralysis of memory. Truly enough, the stars have warned her of the apocalyptic nature of the day, heralding, above all, 'illegal entries'. Against the promise of 'un-invited guests, perhaps bill collectors or insurance salesmen, domineering and resolute', she has chainlocked the entrance to her sanctuary. 'Sagittarius beware', are the first words to greet her over morning tea, 'night-time is closing in upon you even in the crisp light of day. Today your home is your castle and it is sacrosanct. Beware of a dark man who enters during the peak hours of sunlight. Be he secret lover or scourge, your money is unsafe, even rolled inside your hair curlers, even stashed in your deep-freeze.'

Yet it is raining and bleak and the face belongs to a woman.

'Why don't you let me in?'

'None today, thank you.'

The old woman cannot quite close the door. Something in the face is carving out a niche in the rage of her consciousness. The dim stranger perhaps has appeared.

'I'm leaving.'

She undoes the chain.

Seven years of Perfidia slip through in a flash. Tea is served. Silence is manifest. The large house glares empty and unused at her. Only this sitting-room, with its amateur maps of the heavens and zodiacal symbols embroidered on doilies and tablecloths, continues to perform in the house's new aura. The face she stares at is aged and painted, the hair sprayed to a hard fibre and softly blue. Now the cracked orange lips have asked her birthsign and a stunned Taurus responds. The bread-knife-shaved pencil stub proceeds to mark out its triangles on a large disc. Her exact birthdate is gathered from her and the intersecting vertices of several triangles are measured in their distances from a central thumbprint the Taurean is forced to make on the paper. The day, apparently, has dawned bright for her. The rain bisects the curve of her joy at about noon. She will be careless today, she will reveal her secrets to a false spirit who will misuse them. Don't go out of doors. Don't give anything away. Reveal nothing. Drink hot liquids by the pint.

'I need to borrow some of your clothes.'

The old woman has stopped abruptly. Her one good eye now closes in on the figure of a young girl seated before her.

'Do you ever wash?'

'Mother . . .'

'My clothes? What for?'

'I'm going to an affair.'

'A formal affair?'

'I haven't any clothes.'

Mother Munch stands before her French windows and accuses the rain. Outside, somewhere, the plants are drowning and no one will lend a helping hand. She has written to the Authorities, complaining of the character of modern life, but they are too busy to respond. All about her the trees are leaping, lifting their skirts to the stars, and there is no one to care. These nights she hears explosions in the vicinity and no one will tell her their meaning or the extent of the damage. Then too, the night has come crawling in sooner, of late, all to persecute her and keep her prisoner in the new decade. Gunfire awakens her at night and even the War brought no sounds of this kind. And who are the men that will protect the women from assault in the dim gutters? And now the thieves have come in on the wind and steal the very nails from her fitted carpets. The Sun has gone down already, only a noontime for her, and will it ever rise up to meet her again? She must inquire of the Chief of Police.

'Get out.'

'I only want one suit of clothes. I'll never bother you again.'

'Nothing from me. You'll steal nothing from me. I know. It's going round. It's in the neighbourhood.'

The rash begins to crawl over Perfidia's legs and her troll-lover thumps his rubber tail in her eyes. She goes to a cupboard, selects a brown suit at random, a lace hat with glass fruit on top, a pair of stockings. She rolls them together against the rain.

'Perfidia!'

The voice tugs at her sleeve in the doorway. Mother Munch has unearthed a breadknife and holds it, handle first, toward the vanishing figure.

'Take everything. Anything you want. Only, please, cut my throat. Cut my throat.'

The young girl disappears in the rain and the old woman must report a theft. It is in the course of things to do so.

In her basement room, Perfidia has put on the stolen garments and glares at an image of her Mother in the mirror. She cups the protruding shoulder of the jacket, throwing her arm across her mouth. She sucks in at the wrist, wonders of the tight hips and long skirt. Kropotkin will find it out of date and detectable. She must rip out the shoulders, shorten the skirt, cut the fruit from the moth-eaten hat. Before doing this, she sees, for the last time, in her widest eye, the wearing of this garment for Father Munch, returning from his wounds, all through that night, never removed.

Her confinement is celebrated this night by the entire Brigade. She is taken to some dark hovel where she will spend the two nights before her act. She will see or communicate with no one, and only the special emissary of the Brigade will bring her instructions at the final hour. She will be given time only to carry out her objective, not to brood on it. This isolation is the rotten fruit of past miscalculations. There have been too many leaks, too many rents in the fabric of Absolute Security.

She is given a ration of brown rice and water. During the preparatory hours she will be fed excessive doses of sugar to mobilize her force. She is made to wear her Mother's clothes until they are worn naturally. On the final day, her emissary will help her to prepare her face and hair, iron her clothing and lead her to a place where she will collect her explosive device. She is made to consume the classic texts which form the background to her act. She must understand the historical perspective and morality of her intentions. She knows her thrust will be against an institution of oppression and therefore will have no need to question the specific shape of her charge at its moment of illumination.

The 1960s had come upon her in a rush, as had Zimmerman. She had given this decade its peculiar shape through a violent eradication of the previous one. If they had been chained to the mediocrity and hyperboredom of the times, the moment now cried out for detonation. He explained all this to her as he became exposed to the political messages which marked the air like Morse Code. Flashing assassinations and gliding chain-reactive explosions. Electricity and its shocks, an overwhelming tactility and percussion for a world up a blind alley.

But she thought he was all these things already. The specification of it in words cheated him of a certain dynamic to which she had spread her wings. To gather the shape of his anger was to lose its ferocity. He wandered in a perpetual planning-stage of cause and effect, stepping out of its protective skin, now and again, to shatter the brains of public men. And to do this was to leave her in the wake of his new awareness. She had no place in it when docility and silence were her measure.

She had anticipated his move to leave her behind and she drew first fire by walking backward out of his aura. She tossed a hood of silence over him and shrouded his body in the limp cloth of her own. She fell away softly and, in his pride, he imagined he was leaving her. It was necessary for him to be alone and clear in his acts. She said nothing. She gave him nothing but her submission, never a gesture in the holocaust of personality disruption. No barriers, no reefs to crash on, only the calm waters of Nothing to glide. He promised that every time he murdered, it would be her in his eyes. This proved true and soon the dim politics of it eroded him.

And now in her dungeon she sees before her the landscape of the decade as he absconds. The months of catatonia, hovering in hovels, the project of rising to regret again through the taking of a hundred arbitrary lovers. The rampant sexuality of her despair, the force-feeding, the dangerous cliffs over which her body dangles. And, above all, the casual abuse of this body, the willing leap to migraine in its inevitability, the mindless erosion of her contours through skin-picking and excess weight, the tired bending of limbs to sexual assault and acceptance of a thousand unknown fluids in her receptacle. This is a virtual 1960s of effects for her, the rapid alternation of psychic energies and exhaustions. Her rhythm is vague. She feels a flush of freedom and growth, running headlong in pursuit. She gathers up territories of achievement and claims them as part of a new personal myth. She drifts off from the double-edged razor of Zimmerman and Mother Munch. She uncovers the roots of her own industry.

And then she fails, in alternation. She struggles with

belief as she sees around her the sputterings of the human mechanism depleting its own resources. Everywhere the day has run down. She collects these ruins and projects them on a screen before her. She witnesses a disappearance of quality and accepts responsibility for it. She trundles up the faded rags of her breed and vows resurrection. Somewhere in this loss of Zimmerman she gains his fists. On the fifteenth anniversary of her migraine she mounts the blood to her brain and enters the port of destruction. She has accepted the dim purpose of her era, its remaking. She leaps.

However, her tomb now mirrors her disaffection with her thrust. The vitality of commitment is already extinguished and she harbours only the potential mischief of her act. Yet she must struggle with her own nature in its apathy, for Kropotkin has surely found her out with his first look.

The room is cold and dark and she has begun to feel a tickling in her loins. She searches with a candle and finds she is discharging a green substance.

He has entered as she knew he would. If it were known, he would be shot. What gives him the security of her silence, even now, she muses. He sits opposite her. She cannot see his face. It occurs to her in such light she may show him her defiance. If it can be absorbed, without him being witness to it, she can follow it through. She realizes, in the silence, that she has always awaited his instigation. He must speak first.

'You're sapping my attention, Perfidia, haunting my sleep again. I warn you, keep off me.'

In his voice she hears a familiar choking. How easy to remember him without seeing his changeable eyes. She hears, out of another era, the soft collapse of his hair on her belly and remembers the signals of fear. Leather crackles as he shifts in his chair and she smells a ghost clinging in the musky room. Something in him has died and now haunts the moment, a moment she has provoked. She calculates the beginning of his confession and interprets it as an impending assault upon her sex. She understands she has brought this about through her silence.

'It was all clear till you started roaming in my nightmares again.'

He has not moved and she remains calm, but with a cautious thumb planted at her waist, at the edge of her blade. Her tickling is now acute and she equates it with a certain air of poison he has brought into the room. She fails to trace the shape of his protest. Its random aggression inflames her and she feels now she has in fact lived clear of him. There is a new deafness to mock the infections he pours in her ear. One moment of direct contagion helps her to circumnavigate five long years of crawling out of his shade. There is a delicious humming in her head.

'Last night I dreamed I carved my initials in your brain, but you refused to decode the message. You've jumped in where you aren't wanted, Perfidia. The other day I jammed my fingers into you and found you'd been done over while I was away. Don't think I'll let you rest with all this, babe. Every time you trip up in the street, I'll be there to lean on you. Every time you crack, I'll come running with my crowbar to finish the job.'

He has gotten up now and her disappointment is immense. She has lived a solid moment without the freight of his body looming over her, has discovered in his voice a loss of hope, in his breathing, the scarred remains of his passion. He will spoil this by ambling towards her, pretending to engage her, all the while stalking and trembling. His hand, a weight on the darkness, hovers in sexual dilemma, mid-air, a hand which has thrown the circuits of Power into chaos, drawn the riot squads up from their retreats – this hand now descends like a carpet on air. She has come up to meet him, despite the blackness, drawing her switchblade between his thumb and forefinger, the blood spattering her shaven head. She doubles back in swift retreat, thinking he will surely kill her now, her knife at the ready. But he only backs off and waits.

'Why don't you try and finish it. You've done my trigger finger. I can't even reach for the pistol. You'd better do it, Perfidia. One cut means nothing. You know what happens next.'

'I'm not afraid of you any longer.'

'You are afraid to finish me. One cut is nothing, babe. You've got nothing, nothing at all out of it. In two days time, you may be forced to kill, and because you aren't prepared to do it, the Movement will suffer.'

She leans to the stone wall to get her breath. The pain in her loins has brought her to the edge of fire. He is right. She will not be able to kill because she is asleep. This pounding fact has opened a chasm before her and she is falling in it. Against her will, the tears have burst from her. She has never known such pain, even at the worst of her bleedings. His contempt is redoubled as he conceives she has collapsed to her knees in cowardice. Again she fails him, his bride of Frankenstein, gone the female route to passivity.

The pain has swollen to a knot, but she grips her knife in anticipation. Kropotkin feels a nerve of deep embarrassment tingle up his back and then subside. He wishes his feelings at this moment were something more powerful, but he has dried to the combat. He recalls a time, perhaps in another life, when he had threatened to kill her and, in self-defence, she took him in her mouth. He remembers waves of retribution and resentment giving way to the desperate ecstasy of his blast and how, in that rush, he had accepted his own instinct to murder. What had torn and racked his youth and sleep, a throbbing resentment of his life, now shattered in a thrill. And it was Perfidia's pitiful secondhand humanity which had yielded up his secret. She knew every corner of him and the emptiness of her presence in his shade became a crisis for him.

And now the despair returns as he witnesses the further evidence of her mutilation. He cannot retract a shred of it. Despite her fury, he disarms her and pins her fast. He sees he has failed to ravage an already shopworn article and he can never again imagine his body holding dominion over this corpse. Up close, he sees that she sees his eyes leaping at her, but that the suffering there fails to ignite her. It is, for him, because she has learned nothing. He wants to leave a kiss here, but this is not the face for it.

The cold military eyes of the doctor force her to a cruel attention here in the halls of the clinic where she has staggered in torment. He studies the results of the tests in which she has been scraped, smeared, probed, watered. She begs for a sedative, he tells her she must wait. She is near fainting now and wonders at her task, just over twenty-four hours ahead. She must manage to return before her emissary arrives, to avoid suspicion and not put the project in jeopardy.

'You have been with a soldier.'

This is more of a statement than a question and it takes her unawares. The face that confronts her expresses nothing; it is ruled, pragmatic, has watched a decade of unceasing infection in the demise of the contemporary urinary tract.

'No.'

'Come come now. We're not here to play games. I'm trying to help you, Miss Luxemburg.'

'I haven't.'

'You must have been.'

'Why?'

'Because you have been passed a strain of gonococcus which derives from South-East Asia and is generally transmitted by soldiers returning from the front. If you haven't been with a soldier, then this is a chain-reaction begun by one, and you'll be helping to spread an epidemic unless you cooperate.'

'I'm sure it isn't true.'

'The rotten thing is that it only acts as mild gonorrhoea in the male, and most of the men treat it lightly. But I'm afraid its effect on the vaginal tract can be severe. The pain you are now experiencing may well be the beginning of pelvic inflammatory disease, an erosive process in the cervix, uterus, Fallopian tubes and ovaries.'

Through the pain, the calculated measure of his voice has penetrated some deep fear and she finds herself listening, not through her normal haze, but rather through a newly-opened window. She wonders if there is a plot to divert her from her mission, but she knows she has come of her own free will.

'I must warn you of the extreme gravity of this bacteria if it spreads. You would be wise to avoid intercourse until you are cleared (if that's not asking too much), no alcohol or spices and drink lots of liquids. After your stay, you must report to us every forty-eight hours.'

'My "stay"?'

'You'll have to stay with us till tomorrow morning. There is a government regulation on this.'

Perfidia has gone white and cold. She regrets her weakness. Instead of this, she might have stolen her mother's tranquillizers and quickly returned to her sanctuary. She could have borne this pain for two days.

'I'm afraid I can't stay. You see . . .'

'You must, Miss Luxemburg. We have strict orders. We have lovely gardens for you to wander in, you can relax, you won't be kept in a bed. We'll notify your family for you.'

'No. Don't.'

'All right then, we'll keep it confidential.'

She reckons all is not lost. If she can leave in the morning, it will give her several hours before the arrival of her emissary. It may not be noticed at all.

She is given further tests, blood-lettings and injections. For her pain there is morphine, an institutional gown to wrap her in and the door leading to the sprawling lawns of the clinic where she must relax. She walks about in nervous anticipation, and the skin of her fingers is the worse for it. More than anything else, her defiance of Kropotkin is at stake. This now overrides any shred of political commitment as her explosive striking-force. It is to shatter his Look in her blast that she lives for her moment of detonation. She gathers the hatred of him, in her catastrophe of pain, and calculates bringing him up on charges, before the Brigade, of entering her confinement and of attempting to block the mission through acts of psychic provocation.

She doesn't quite remember how she has sunk to the grass, can't recall a sudden short circuit. The current stopped and she fell through gravitational space in desperate free-fall, the forces of her delirium tugged her windward and the echo of her thud informed a distracted earth of her affliction.

Now the Sun relates a spectacle in the midst of which she is released from her coma. She is aware first of a sense of space, vast and green, and she is shaken from the traps of her confinement. Despite the sterility of the grounds, she finds a benevolence here in the languid shrubbery of the afternoon. Slowly her body drifts out of its morphine shell and the pains begin to mount again; yet, she is calm. Somewhere, somehow, she feels that a crisis has passed or is just passing. It is the delicious twilight leave-taking of morphine. Her hand reaches beneath her gown and returns to her a pale green. Between her legs a ravaged city is undergoing a post-war experience. She replaces her fingers and drives them slowly upward, through the walls of the fortress, into the thick of its devastation. There is no life anymore, only an aftermath, only the taint of plague everywhere. A soldier. She recalls no soldiers. And yet how many invading armies have rampaged in these town Walls, taken into the sanctuary indiscriminately? Her recollection is poor. But now the streets are flowing in a sewage of green mucus, left by some faceless minister of infection. And, too, the hallowed halls at her depths are charred and scourged, the insides of her humanity shredded and running green. This is a woman's disaster, she muses, and, in some curious woman's despair and anguish, she has willed it.

Perfidia sits up as best she can and the blood rushes into

her belly, out of her brain, the empty chasm where her troll-lover waits to take his place. She experiences the failure of her body. It has dredged up its wastes and stored them in her awkward corners, forcing her to walk or stand in perpetual muscular discomfort and confusion. Before her she conjures up her spectre of achievement, of action in the provocative mirrors of the world. She knows now, in a brief moment of suspended clarity lighting up the broken hours of her days, that she lacks the grace she needs to set these fires under her.

All this is a clamour in her ears. A tide of years is surging in her and threatening a flood of regret over the dam she has built against herself. She must collect and face the time.

But in this composure-seeking a public man has approached and stands over her. He smiles casually, but she has been trained to recognize a certain disciplinary eye. He would like a few words with her and, in his laboured politeness, he has carelessly identified himself with strategies of law. He explains again the routine of detaining patients suffering from this ailment. Perfidia further wakes to a situation of extreme alarm and she regrets she cannot muster the control to deal with this sudden preponderance of authority. Could she please identify the soldier she has been with? She again denies the existence of such a man. Has she, he begs her pardon, slept with anyone of late who has slept with someone who has slept, might have slept, with a soldier? She has slept with no one. Nonetheless, he reminds her, she has contracted, as he calls it, 'a social disease'. It must have come from somewhere. Women can pick up such infections without intercourse, she informs him. Not this one, she is told. To be perfectly honest, says the policeman or whatever he may be in his crisp black suit, all servicemen returning from 'that part of the world' are subjected to strict urinalysis and none is released until 'clear'. She misses the implication. It's quite simple, he explains, the man who has left her in this dilemma has not been through the normal medical channels, which is highly irregular, illegal and impossible except in cases of absence without official leave. Perfidia is lost in this, implicated, as she is, in one of her own nightmares, and the paranoia is acute. She knows nothing, she pleads. Remember, he warns, who you are, Miss Munch. And now the snare is truly laid as she reads his face precisely. It registers every step she has taken for three months, every petty theft, knows her connections, her plans for the immediate future, has informed on the very dirt beneath her fingernails.

'We can discuss it further tomorrow.'

He stands, carefully brushes the grass from his legs.

'Tomorrow?'

'Oh yes, you aren't leaving here, Perfidia. It's all over, you know.'

That night she is subjected to more probing in her city laid waste. Every entry brings with it great pain and sensation, all quite new to her. She is given morphine and, as she fades, she explores herself again, discovering new furrows, new valleys and waterways. It occurs to her she is fighting for her life. Not against the riot squads and their smiling executives, or even Kropotkin and his pressure, but against the years, the years which have climbed on her, probed, scraped, left her as broken glass under their immense weight.

She is riding to sleep on the crest of her disaster. The clinic has become an instant prison into which she will wake in chains.

In the night she dreams of her escape across the panorama of green, shearing the barbed wire as Kropotkin has taught in his lectures. She cannot cross the city in her hospital gown or she will raise suspicion. Instead, she makes her way to Mother Munch's, enters and rifles her wardrobes. Something startles her in the act and behind her stands the old woman with her breadknife. She has always faced her facelessly, hoping to remove herself from the elder's gaze. She has made chaos of her Mother's intentions. She ought, she feels, to be ashamed. But this time she can hold a stare; it states her case.

The breadknife cuts through the hospital garment and the old woman amuses herself with the naked body of this young girl, unwashed and curiously without eyebrows or hair. She can recognize contours in this body out of some obscure memory. With her long fingernails she draws blood on the girl's breast and elicits the scream which has hung suspended over the years. Her response is a cackle and Perfidia understands she has become a witch. From out of the marshes of her misery she has pulled forth a sort of madness, and built on it a viable ending for her life. She dabbles, these days, in the stars, finding puzzles and mythologies which bear her dying body along the roads of magic. She has turned her grief to mystic advantage and Perfidia feels a new and secret bond with this gipsy. Across her charts, she seems to be calling her to revolt, to ride the wind and accept the darkness of the days.

But she has merely come for the costumes. She dresses, again in the trappings of the 1940s and, as she turns to leave, presents the old woman with a vision of younger times, a recognition of her 'soul' at the peripheries of its decay. To kiss each other now would be a gesture to sentiment designed to obscure their new covenant. Instead, the Mother has turned back to her triangles in a heat and the daughter has fled to her upheavals in a flash.

The threatening eyes of her emissary greet her in the cellar. Perfidia has calculated plenty of time before the event, but she is informed that the manoeuvre has been put forward, indeed, is imminent. Can she explain her disappearance? Not now. She is ready to perform. There is no room for dialogue; the performance is all.

She dresses, paints her face, puts on a blond wig. In the hazy mirror she has become her Mother.

The emissary now drives her, in a van with black windows, to a room where she will collect her explosive device. Then she is told she will take her bomb to an electrical works on the city's perimeter, carry it in a handbag and leave it in a second-floor Ladies Toilet. Perfidia asks if she must wait until the building is cleared. On the contrary, she is told, this bomb must take lives. When she sees the face of Kropotkin behind the device, she knows it is his decision. He stares at her absently as he sets the time mechanism and hands her the package. Before she leaves he goes to her and adjusts her wig, then hands her a folded piece of tissue paper in which she finds two eyebrows.

On the way, she understands at last the gravity of her objective. She is called upon to disrupt the power, to turn institutional murder in upon itself. Yet, she must constantly adjust the wig, which the hands of Kropotkin have thrown into permanent disarray. She feels unclean and the cake of her face weighs on her cheeks like cloth. It occurs to her she is without her knife, lost somewhere perhaps in the gardens of the clinic or taken by the investigating policeman.

At the gates of the intended building she is struck by migraine.

She walks through the gaze of the Security Guard, explaining that she has come to see her husband, a certain Mr Y. who works in the plant, no, there is no need to call him, she knows the way, lovely new carpets (she has been told to say), whatever happened to nice Mr D. who worked as a guard last year – to establish an identity.

She places the bomb with five minutes to spare. She goes to the mirror, a woman's mirror in a woman's white porcelain room, and in it discovers an eyebrow dangling from the outside of her eye like a worm. She knows, in the feel of it, that it has been so for some time.

Outside the door she hears voices, and her failure is written on the night. The explosion is now three minutes away and she freezes at her edges. In her head a pulse, like the slow crack of the sea, is gathering its thunder. She rushes to the sink and washes her face clean of its mildew. Also, she scrubs her neck of its rust, watching the bomb-lever twist closer to holocaust. As the towel unveils, in its drying, a chalky whiteness stares back at her. Voices are mumbling at the door in anticipation, she hears the running of feet, the shrill echo of police whistles. She feels she is gaining a laceration in the heart of Power. Will she gain the Power? She doesn't know.

Again she tries her mirror. The face she sees has accepted nothing, wants nothing. It watches the explosive in its final minute, now the ticking is her troll-lover, prodding her with his sex. They are pounding on the door for her to come out, smiling killer police who will not enter a lady's sanctuary for their embarrassment. It is the world of their embarrassment and its antiface, their brutality, she must unmake. Without eyebrows, if necessary.

No. She does not want the Power, and she leaps. The policeman, the same who has incarcerated her, catches her as she pushes into the hallway. She fights against him for cover. She wants, she thinks, to live. She tries to warn him of the bomb, but he holds her mouth fast because women bite. Women do such things.

She hears a crack, two, three, and the policeman falls from her. Kropotkin stands over them with his pistol and strips the dead man of his identity card to add to his collection. He appears unconcerned about the bomb and indeed the ticking has stopped and there is no explosion.

'It was a test.'

She fumbles in her narcosis and dreams now of Kropotkin's grin on the day of his execution. Her masses of hair tumble behind her as she rides to the secluded wood on her bicycle. These are the woods of the 1940s where her Mother has described the lurkings of rape and masturbation and now, as then, she drifts to them in fascination. The willows overhang the small ponds polluted now with dead frogs where she once walked with Father Munch when the War had ended, as they say. In this thickness she has discovered her secret anguish and kept it to herself, for herself. All the dreadful mini-deaths of the woman she has unlocked here.

And Father Munch walks here no more. The world is without men once again and the crackle of times long ago is with her.

She comes upon a lake and swims in it naked to limber her body and, on its banks, she performs her ballet lessons, thrusting her legs to the air in postures of angular composure. Her dance is private and yet the world holds its breath in the camouflaging leaves.

She finds the sisters in the appointed place and a calm Kropotkin, manacled to a tree, blows her a mocking kiss. She has kept them waiting, is reprimanded and finally asked to carry out her task. She is handed his own pistol and she goes to him at his tree. He looks up as she holds the gun to his head, challenging her in a final moment. A softness, like hair, touches her in her secret places and a laughter overwhelms her. She sits down by a pool, with her feet in the cool water. A sister collects the gun from her as Kropotkin shrieks her enduring weakness to the decades. He goes to his death believing this as the sister spatters his brains about the forest. Perfidia, smiling back over her shoulder, no longer feels the need to bury his eyes separately and far away. There is nothing to live up to, nothing at all to prove.

Biographical Notes

Kingsley Amis

was born in Clapham in 1922 and educated at the City of London School and St John's College, Oxford. At the age of eleven he embarked on a blank-verse miniature epic at the instigation of a secondary-school master, and has been writing verse ever since. Until the age of twenty-four, however, he remarks: 'I was in all departments of writing *abnormally unpromising.*' With James Michie he edited *Oxford Poetry 1949.* Until 1963 he was a university teacher of English; he is a keen science-fiction addict, an admirer of 'white jazz' of the thirties and the author of articles and reviews in most of the leading papers and periodicals. His novels are *Lucky Jim* (1954), *That Uncertain Feeling* (1955), *I Like it Here* (1958), *Take a Girl Like You* (1960), *One Fat Englishman* (1963), *The Anti-death League* (1966), *I Want it Now* (1968), *The Green Man* (1969) and *Girl, 20* (1971). He has also written a book of short stories, *My Enemy's Enemy* (1962), *The Egyptologists* (1965) with Robert Conquest, *Colonel Sun* (1968) under a pseudonym, *New Maps of Hell,* (1960) a survey of science fiction, *The James Bond Dossier* (1965), and *What Became of Jane Austen?*, essays and reviews (1970). His collections of poetry are *A Frame of Mind* (1953), *A Case of Samples* (1956) and *A Look Round the Estate* (1967). Some of his poems are published in *Penguin Modern Poets 2.* He has two sons and a daughter. He is married to the novelist Elizabeth Jane Howard.

Biographical Notes

Ruth Prawer Jhabvala

was born of Polish parents in Cologne, Germany, in 1927, and came to England with her family in 1939. She went to Hendon County School, and took an M.A. in English from London University. In 1951 she married an Indian architect, C. S. H. Jhabvala, and went to live in Delhi where she has made her home. She has three daughters. She has published six novels: *To Whom She Will, The Nature of Passion, Esmond in India, The Householder, Get Ready for Battle* and *A Backward Place*; and three collections of much praised short stories. Her novel *The Householder* has been filmed, and she has written four screenplays with James Ivory, including *The Guru* and the much loved *Shakespeare Wallah.*

David Zane Mairowitz

was born in New York City in 1943. He studied English literature and philosophy at Hunter College, New York, and drama at the University of California, Berkeley. Trained as a Director, he worked in theatres in California and the Midwest. He came to England in 1966 where he has lived chiefly ever since, except for brief periods in Denmark and France. He is at present working on a book about American Experience as seen from the point of view of exile in a 'reticent' culture. He was among the founding editors of the International Times (IT), and has had two plays performed in London at the Open Space Theatre, *The Law Circus* (1969), and *Flash Gordon and the Angels* (1971). He had edited *BAMN: Outlaw Manifestos and Ephemera 1965–70* for Penguin (1971) and writes occasionally for Scandinavian and American periodicals, including the *Village Voice*. He says he has no intention of living in the US in the forseeable future. These stories form part of a collection entitled *Failures.*

More about Penguins

Penguinews, which appears every month, contains details of all the new books issued by Penguins as they are published. From time to time it is supplemented by *Penguins in Print,* which is a complete list of all available books published by Penguins. (There are well over three thousand of these.)

A specimen copy of *Penguinews* will be sent to you free on request, and you can become a subscriber for the price of the postage. For a year's issues (including the complete lists) please send 30p if you live in the United Kingdom, or 60p if you live elsewhere. Just write to Dept EP, Penguin Books Ltd, Harmondsworth, Middlesex, enclosing a cheque or postal order, and your name will be added to the mailing list.

Note: *Penguinews* and *Penguins in Print* are not available in the U.S.A. or Canada

The Penguin Book of English Short Stories

Edited by Christopher Dolley

Some of the stories in this collection – such as Wells's *The Country of the Blind* and Joyce's *The Dead* – are classics; others – like Dickens's *The Signalman* and Lawrence's *Fanny and Annie* – are less well known. But all of them – whether funny, tragic, wry or fantastic – show their authors at their concise best. Which makes this representative collection, at the very least, ferociously entertaining. An Open University Set Book

Not for sale in the U.S.A.

The Penguin Book of American Short Stories

Edited by James Cochrane

This collection offers twenty-one short stories from the literature of America, a nation which has always been particularly at home in this form, and which has produced many of its masters. Some of the stories included – those by Poe, James and Hemingway for example – are already widely known. Some of the others will be less familiar to the English reader. The collection as a whole should serve as an introduction to the rich diversity of pleasures that the American short story at its best can offer.

Not for sale in the U.S.A.

Penguin Parallel Texts

French Short Stories

Edited by Pamela Tomlinson

The eight short stories in this collection, by Marcel
Aymé, Alain Robbe-Grillet, Raymond Queneau and other
French writers, have been selected both for their literary
merit and as being representative of contemporary
French writing. The English translations which are
printed in a parallel text are literal rather than literary,
and there are notes and biographies of the authors.
The volume is primarily intended to help English-
speaking students of French, but these stories stand on
their own and make excellent reading in either language.

Soviet Short Stories

Edited by Richard Newnham

The eight stories in this collection have been chosen both
for their interest as contemporary Soviet literature and
for the light they throw on Soviet attitudes to such
subjects as officialdom, youth, art, and recent history. For
the general reader, they are also chosen to give some
indication of the highly variable quality of Soviet writing
today – a factor which Western collections have tended to
ignore.
All the stories, which range from 1929 to 1961, have been
specially translated for this edition. The Russian texts on
facing pages, and the detailed notes and biographies, will
help the student to gain confidence in his reading as well
as a more realistic sense of the value of learning the
language.

Penguin Parallel Texts

Italian Short Stories

Edited by Raleigh Trevelyan

The eight stories in this collection, by Moravia, Pavese, Pratolini, and other modern writers, have been selected as being representative of contemporary Italian writing. The English translations provided are literal rather than literary, and there are notes and biographies of the writers to help the student of Italian. However, the volume can also be helpful to Italians, who can improve their English by studying a strict rendering of stories with which they may already be familiar.

German Short Stories

Edited by Richard Newnham

The eight short stories in this collection are representative of post-war authors whose work has been published in West Germany. Parallel texts in German and English, together with notes and biographies, are provided.

Short Stories in Spanish

Edited by Jean Franco

The stories selected are representative of contemporary writing in Spanish from all parts, and seven of the eight included are the work of Spanish-American authors.

Penguin Modern Stories

Penguin Modern Stories is published quarterly and consists of short stories by new writers as well as by established practitioners of the genre.

1* William Sansom Jean Rhys David Plante
Bernard Malamud

2* John Updike Sylvia Plath Emanuel Litvinoff

3† Philip Roth Margaret Drabble Jay Neugeboren
Giles Gordon

4† Sean O'Faolain Nadine Gordimer Shiva Naipaul
Isaac Babel

5† Penelope Gilliat Benedict Kiely Andrew Travers
Anthony Burton

6† Elizabeth Taylor Dan Jacobson Maggie Ross
Robert Nye

7† Anthony Burgess Susan Hill Yehuda Amichai
B. S. Johnson

8† William Trevor C. J. Driver A. L. Barker

9† V. S. Pritchett Ruth Fainlight Frederick Busch
Mel Calman

10* Brian Glanville Janice Elliott Jennifer Dawson
Paul Winstanley Jean Stubbs

Not for sale in the U.S.A.

†*Not for sale in the U.S.A. or Canada*